EL BRONX

BOOKS BY JEROME CHARYN

EL BRONX

LITTLE ANGEL STREET

MONTEZUMA'S MAN

BACK TO BATAAN

MARIA'S GIRLS

ELSINORE

THE GOOD POLICEMAN

MOVIELAND

PARADISE MAN

METROPOLIS

WAR CRIES OVER AVENUE C

PINOCCHIO'S NOSE

PANNA MARIA

DARLIN' BILL

THE CATFISH MAN

THE SEVENTH BABE

SECRET ISAAC

THE FRANKLIN SCARE

THE EDUCATION OF PATRICK SILVER

MARILYN THE WILD

BLUE EYES

THE TAR BABY

EISENHOWER, MY EISENHOWER

AMERICAN SCRAPBOOK

GOING TO JERUSALEM

THE MAN WHO GREW YOUNGER

ON THE DARKENING GREEN

ONCE UPON A DROSHKY

EDITED BY JEROME CHARYN

THE NEW MYSTERY

EL BRONX

JEROME CHARYN

THE MYSTERIOUS PRESS

Published by Warner Books

A Time Warner Company

This book is a work of fiction. Names, characters, places and incidents are the product of the author's imagination or are used fictitiously. Any resemblance to actual events, locales or persons, living or dead, is coincidental.

 Mysterious Press books are published by Warner Books, Inc., 1271 Avenue of the Americas, New York, NY 10020.

 A Time Warner Company

The Mysterious Press name and logo are registered trademarks of Warner Books, Inc.

Printed in the United States of America

First Printing: February 1997

10 9 8 7 6 5 4 3 2 1

Library of Congress Cataloging-in-Publication Data

Charyn, Jerome.
    El Bronx / Jerome Charyn.
        p.   cm.
    ISBN 0-89296-604-1
    I. Title.
    PS3553.H33B76   1997
    813'.54—dc20

96-24755
CIP

Part One

1

It was open season. America was in the middle of a baseball war . . . and a wildcat strike. The players had their own private czar, J. Michael Storm, who was much more powerful than the commissioner and the presidents of both leagues. He would only talk to one guy. Isaac Sidel, the mayor of New York, had to become a middleman in a war he didn't want. J. Michael would fly in from Houston, where he had his law firm, but he wouldn't meet with Isaac at Gracie Mansion. He would ride up to Yankee Stadium with Sidel, sit with him in the owners' box, look at the deserted playing field and start to crow.

"Empty houses, Isaac, that's what I see."

"And we'll all be losers . . . come on, J. Michael, can't I go to the owners with a proposition, let's say a cap of ten million dollars?"

"No salary cap. It's a form of slavery."

"Slavery at ten million a year? That's sixty-one thousand seven hundred and twenty-eight dollars and forty fucking cents per game."

"Stop throwing numbers. It's the principle of the thing. I can't negotiate when the price tag's been rigged."

"Crybaby," Isaac said. "Didn't you demand a minimum wage?"

"That's different. A boy could crack his arm and never play again. He's got to have a nest egg."

Isaac started to pace like a wild animal in the owners' box. He was the landlord here. The Yankees rented from him. "J., you're not leaving the premises until I get a commitment from you."

J. Michael Storm started to laugh. "Are you going to glock me?" he said, pointing to the big black gun in Isaac's pants.

"I'll do worse than that. I'll throw you out the window."

"I'd come bouncing right off the grass."

He was a student radical at Columbia when Isaac met him twenty years ago; the son of kindergarten teachers, he'd come up from the South to play Raskolnikov in the big city. Isaac had been his own kind of Raskolnikov, a young chief in the First Deputy's office who seemed more comfortable around Mafia dons than his own captains. He'd kept J. Michael out of jail, debated with him at student societies, talked about Plato and Karl Marx. When J. Michael and his Ho Chi Minh Club seized the president's office at Low Library, held the president hostage for half a day, it was Isaac who went into Low, talked to the Ho Chi Minhs and freed the president, who wouldn't press charges against any of the radicals.

"J., the Bronx is gonna die. It can't survive without the Yanks. This stadium is the last fucking lubrication that's left in the whole South Bronx. Should I tell you the income it brings in? I'm not talking ticket sales. I'm talking about the little shops along Jerome Avenue, the parking lot people, the hot-dog vendors . . ."

"Isaac, you're breaking my heart."

"What happened to the son of Ho?"

"I left him inside my graduation gown. Isaac, I represent a couple hundred millionaires. None of them was born with a silver spoon in his ass. They're homeboys, like you and me. And they're not gonna starve. They can wait out every single owner in organized baseball. And if the going's rough, I can get them fat contracts to play ball in Japan."

"Yeah, more and more gaijins on the Yokohama Giants."

Marvin Hatter, the Yankees' president, came into the box. "Can I get you boys anything? Champagne and wild strawberries?"

"You're not supposed to spy on us, Marve," J. Michael said. "I can have the courts haul you out of here."

"This is my ball club, Mr. Storm. You and the mayor are guests."

"Wrong. You rent from Isaac . . . now get the fuck out of here, Marve."

The Yankees' president disappeared from the box, helpless against this whirlwind, who suddenly dropped his head inside his hands. "Isaac, I'm losing my little girl." His wife, Clarice, had moved to Manhattan with their daughter, a twelve-year-old beauty named Marianna Storm. Isaac was very fond of the girl, who would visit him at Gracie Mansion.

"You're her father. Take her to lunch."

"I can't. Clarice has poisoned her against me."

"I won't mediate between you and Clarice. I have a baseball war on my hands."

"But you could sneak me into your club."

"What club, J. Michael? The Ho Chi Minhs?"

"That fucking cultural enrichment program—Magician, or something."

"Merlin, you mean."

Isaac was always rushing into other people's terrains. He couldn't build his own board of education, and so he started a satellite, a school away from school, where kids from the worst bombed-out areas of the Bronx could meet little wizards from the gold coast of Manhattan and Brooklyn Heights. But he couldn't tell who the real wizards were, who was *enriching* whom, the ghetto kids or the gold coasters. Isaac had recruited Marianna Storm, who sat in her tower on Sutton Place South and had never even been to the Bronx.

"J.," Isaac said, "I can't sneak you in. It wouldn't be ethical. I'd betray Marianna's trust if I let her own dad start to dog her."

J. Michael took out an enormous checkbook from a pocket under his heart and scribbled a check for fifty thousand dollars, payable to "Merlin/Isaac Sidel." Isaac stared at the piece of paper and pulled out his Glock. "You have the right to remain silent . . ."

"What the fuck are you doing, Sidel?"

"Arresting you. I'm a public servant, J. You can't start bribing me in my own town."

"I made a contribution to your little club . . . and how can you arrest me? You're only the fucking mayor."

"I have all the powers of a constable," Isaac said. He put his gun back inside his pants and tore up the check with a tiny groan. Merlin was bankrupt, and Isaac was desperate for cash, but he couldn't allow J. Michael to compromise him, create his own power base inside Merlin.

The players' czar suddenly lost all interest in Sidel. He had a television date downtown. Could he drop the mayor off somewhere? Isaac decided to remain in the Bronx.

"You're a disappointment to me, J. I preferred that kid with the mustache in the president's office."

"And you should have let me go to jail. Because I'm not giving you the Bronx. The Yankees can join the dinosaurs' league. This stadium is dead."

"Why, J.?"

"Because I'm a son of a bitch . . . adios."

J. Michael dug a Yankee cap out of his pocket, unfolded it, put it on his skull, winked, and left Isaac all alone in the wilds of Yankee Stadium, he who'd grown up with DiMaggio and Charlie "King Kong" Keller, and the Dutchman, Tommy Henrich, could *feel* them through the glass, see them in their phantom positions, the Yankees of fifty years ago. He'd been a Giant fan, but he couldn't afford sentimental attachments. He had to save the Bronx.

He walked out of that deserted bowl, through the players' gate, which a guard opened for him, visited with the shopkeepers along Jerome Avenue, most of whom already had black ribbons in their windows. They were mourning the Yanks and marking their own inability to survive.

"Hang on," Isaac said, "we'll find a way."

He walked deeper into the Bronx, entered a crackhouse full of nine-year-old kids, their fingers and lips all burnt from the hot pipes in their hands.

"You gonna light up with us, pappy?" their leader said. "It'll cost you fifteen."

"Why fifteen?" Isaac asked, looking at their grim and greedy faces.

"Because you have to lease our pipe and pay for protection."

Isaac began to cry. How could he help such ferocious capitalists?

"Ah, nobody's gonna rob you, grandpa," they said, pitying this polar bear who'd wandered into their den. Then they saw the Glock in his pants. They took out enormous butcher knives that they kept under a blanket. They could hardly swing the knives, which shivered in their hands.

"You tryin' to steal our works?"

"Ah, have a heart," Isaac said and walked out of that little cave in the Bronx . . .

He returned to Gracie Mansion. Marianna Storm was in the kitchen, baking cookies for Isaac. She'd come uptown to visit him after school, the most devoted member of Merlin, a blond beauty with sea green eyes.

"I was with your dad this afternoon," Isaac said.

"I know."

"He wouldn't talk baseball. He offered to finance Merlin if I could help him get to see you."

"And what did you tell him, Isaac?"

"To scratch himself. I started to read him his rights . . . nobody bribes me. But how could I arrest the players' representative? We'd never end the strike. That still doesn't explain why you won't see him."

"Isaac, don't be brutal. He hired somebody to kill Clarice."

"I don't believe it," Isaac said. "J. Michael loves you. He wouldn't make his own little girl into an orphan."

"He could console himself," Marianna said. "He'd have mama's millions."

"The man has millions of his own."

"Not anymore. Daddy has expensive tastes. I'm richer than he is at the moment."

"But why didn't your mother go to the police?"

"She doesn't like cops. And she doesn't want them to meddle in family business."

"But she could have come to me. I'll break J. Michael's legs."

"That's what she's afraid of. You're much too emotional. She'll cut Daddy to ribbons with her team of lawyers."

"I don't care. You can't hire a hitter in my town and get away with it."

"Isaac, it happens every day." She put on a pair of

insulated gloves and guided the cookie pan out of the oven. They were from Marianna's private recipe. Mocha chip, with walnuts. She'd bake them in batches of a hundred, but Isaac could never get enough. He wouldn't share them with his deputies, only with the baker herself.

"You're not to talk to Mom about the hit man, Isaac, do you promise?"

"How can I promise something like that?"

"Isaac, what if I stopped baking you cookies?"

"I'd be a very unhappy man. But . . ."

"I'll keep you informed," she said, putting on her coat.

"Where are you going? We haven't had our coffee yet."

"I'm not supposed to drink coffee. I'm twelve years old. The caffeine will give me palpitations."

"Then why do you keep begging me for a cup?"

"Because I like to get my way . . . I'm late for my aikido class, if you have to know."

"Aikido," Isaac said, jealous that this little girl had her own martial-arts master . . . and a wooden sword which she kept in a cotton scabbard that she carried under her arm. She pecked Isaac on the cheek and ran out of the mansion with her sword. Isaac was miserable. He couldn't have Marianna's company and he couldn't save the Bronx. He gobbled all the cookies like a gluttonous bear. The cookies were his consolation prize. And he trudged up the stairs to his bedroom with the worst bellyache in his life.

2

He had a million things to do in the morning. Isaac sneaked downstairs at dawn and made his own cappuccino. He couldn't function without the smell of coffee beans and burnt milk. His deputies arrived before eight, and Isaac had none of Marianna's cookies to offer them. They convened in the living room, while Harvey, the mayor's valet, brewed a pot of American coffee and prepared scrambled eggs in a silver chafing dish. The budget director was there with Martha Dime, Corporation Counsel (the City's own lawyer); Victor Sanchez, who was in charge of the Bronx Sheriff's Office; Nicholas Bright, first deputy mayor, who oversaw the City for Isaac Sidel, ran it day by day; Candida Cortez, deputy mayor for finance, who planned the City's economic strategies and watched over its bank accounts; and they all tasted Harvey's scrambled eggs. The mayor had a chef, but she was mediocre, and Isaac had put Mathilde in charge of the laundry room.

He didn't have the capacity to fire people. He simply rotated them, had them become pieces in his own elaborate game of musical chairs.

The last musical chair arrived late. Rebecca Karp, éminence grise of the Sidel administration, and the least popular mayor New York had ever had. Sidel wouldn't make a move without her. He'd served as police commissioner under Becky Karp, had slept with her—City pols nicknamed them "Isis and Osiris," the sister and brother act—and he let her keep one of the back bedrooms. But Rebecca seldom slept at the mansion. She didn't want to spoil Isaac's popularity, play the bad sister.

Isaac had asked them here to help him stop the hemorrhaging of the Bronx. Queens could survive with a dead ballpark; it had its own film studio, its own golf links and tennis lawns, its own bread factories and airports, its own electricity plant, its own racetrack; the Bronx had Yankee Stadium.

"Fucking Robert Moses," Isaac muttered. Moses, New York's master builder, had split the Bronx in two, ploughed across entire neighborhoods to put up an expressway in the 1950s along the borough's spine, and everything east of the expressway had begun to rot and die.

"Isaac," Rebecca hissed, with coffee swirling between her teeth. "Don't give me your funeral face. We can't undo what Moses has done."

"And should I listen to the bankers, Rebecca darling, and say, 'Forget about El Bronx. It's filled with Latinos on welfare, crack babies, infants with AIDS.'"

"Isaac," Rebecca said, "where are the bankers? Shouldn't they be with us?"

"I didn't invite them."

"And where's Billy the Kid?"

Billy the Kid was governor of New York, and chairman of the Financial Control Board, which sat like a bird of prey over New York City. Isaac was also on that board, but Billy ruled it. Billy the Kid was making a run for the White House, and he didn't want to be saddled with a sick borough. El Bronx couldn't generate any money for his campaign chest. Its voters were unpredictable. They were liable to go against Billy and get into a Republican mood.

"I won't have him eating eggs at my table. Billy's no friend of baseball. He'd love to prolong the strike. He'll step in at the last moment and play the angel who pleaded with J. Michael to end the war."

"But Isaac," said Candida Cortez, "we can't save the Bronx without the bankers and Billy the Kid."

"Yes we can."

"How?" asked Victor Sanchez. "Do we put out a contract on J. Michael Storm, or do we whack him ourselves?"

"It's not a bad idea."

Rebecca groaned. "Talk murder, Isaac. It will look lovely in the minutes."

"There are no minutes . . . it's an informal gathering. Coffee and eggs."

"Breakfast's nice, but if we can't bring back the Yanks, sonny boy, there won't be a Bronx."

"We could economize in the meantime," said Martha

Dime. "Close a hospital, merge a couple of day-care centers."

"Not a chance," said the mayor.

"Isaac, we can't work miracles. The numbers don't match," said Candida Cortez. "You think I like it? There were wild dogs in Crotona Park when I was a kid. My dad had to shoot them with his own gun. But the dogs are coming back . . ."

"I'll rip their hearts out," Isaac said.

"We wouldn't let you into the park," said Nicholas Bright. "It would be an insurance risk. You'd cost the City a hundred thousand dollars a day if you're hospitalized."

"How come? That's much too high."

"It takes ten people to cover for you when you're incapacitated. You'd need bodyguards and nurses around the clock . . . Your Honor, speaking for the City, I forbid you to go into Crotona Park."

"All right," Isaac said, "I won't go hunting wild dogs. But ladies and gentlemen, the wild dogs will soon be hunting us."

Isaac walked out on the deputies, but he had one of his bodyguards drive him downtown to Clarice Storm. Clarice had her own security system, a pair of bodyguards who frisked Isaac and made him leave his Glock on the mantel.

"I'm the mayor," Isaac had to plead. "I don't commit crimes."

"He's a liar," someone shouted from the terrace. It was Clarice, clutching a vodka glass at nine in the morning. She was naked under a robe which had the mark of a hotel in Madrid. Clarice loved to steal bits of treasure as she hopped from hotel to hotel: towels, bathrobes, velvet slippers. She was seventeen when J. Michael married her, a senior at some fancy finishing school outside Abilene, and she'd remained a child bride who lived on vodka and potato chips.

Clarice growled at her bodyguards and guzzled the vodka. "Isaac, did you come here to crawl into my bed?"

"Not quite. Marianna was at the mansion yesterday and—"

"Isaac, I'm warning you, I won't discuss my own child this early in the morning. Be a dear, and get another bottle out of the freezer."

"I'm not your vodka boy."

"Then scram. I didn't ask for you, Mr. Mayor. Don't worry, I won't abandon your little Merlins. You can still use my penthouse to meet with those brainchildren . . . what did Marianna say?"

"That J. Michael wants you dead."

"Isn't that what most husbands want? He's sick of me, or I'm sick of him. I can't remember which came first."

"That he went as far as hiring a hitter."

Clarice was suddenly alert; the vodka seemed to drain out of her eyes. "She shouldn't have told you that. It's a wild guess."

"Is that why you have two bodyguards with their own Glocks?"

"It's all in the family, Isaac. They're protecting me from J. Michael. If you'd come for coffee last month, you would have seen a rather large mouse under my eye. A gift from J. He'd like me to break one of Marianna's trusts. The baseball czar is short of cash."

"And having you killed gets him onto the gravy train?"

"Almost. He can amuse himself with Marianna's money, collect on a couple of insurance policies, raid our joint accounts."

"Not after a homicide. The courts won't release a penny to him."

"And what if this phantom hitter makes it look like an accident . . . or a suicide? Worthless, drunken wife takes a flying leap off her own terrace."

"But I'll know about it, and I'll haunt J. Michael . . . Clarice, I can lend you my son-in-law, Barbarossa. He's with Special Services. I think he's guarding Madonna at the moment. I can pull him off that detail."

"No cops . . . my boys have their orders. Shoot to kill."

"That's part of the problem. They could get trigger-happy. And then the cops will be all over the place . . . tell me about the hitter."

"There isn't that much to tell. He snuck into my bedroom, before I hired Milton and Sam. I was in my usual vodka haze. He smoked a cigarette, sat beside me, then picked me up, and carried me toward the terrace. He was rather gentle, really."

"What did he look like? Did you catch his face?"

"Don't be silly. Would he smoke a cigarette if I could see his face? He was wearing a hood."

"Hood?" Isaac asked. "You mean a stocking mask."

"Not at all. An old-fashioned hood, like hangmen used to wear, with eyeholes and a tiny slit for his mouth."

"Fantômas," Isaac muttered to himself.

"Who's Fantômas? I never met him."

"The king of crime," Isaac said. "A character out of a couple dozen books. I used to make all my students read about Fantômas when I taught at the Academy. He could corrupt entire police departments, play a police chief . . . he's the guy who stands right in front of chaos. He was very fond of masks and hoods."

"And you think my friend with the hood was another Fantômas?"

"How should I know? He was carrying you toward the terrace, and then what happened?"

"Marianna stumbled into my room. Fantômas stopped, put me down. I could hear him hiss."

"Marianna saw him?"

"I think so. She couldn't have missed Fantômas."

"And he walked out? Why didn't you call the doorman, have him stopped?"

"Isaac, Fantômas doesn't like doors. He climbed down the terrace wall, disappeared."

"Like a fucking jewel thief . . . Clarice, if he has access to your balcony, if he can come and go like that, it doesn't matter how many bodyguards you have. He holds the key to your fort. Get out of here, move."

"And give up Fantômas?"

"It isn't a joke. Marianna might not be around next time. And that hitter will push you over the wall."

"Or sleep with me. Isaac, I can read eyeholes. Fantô-mas was turned on."

"Yeah, yeah, isn't that what all the philosophers say? Sex and death are the same thing . . . suppose he sleeps with you and then sends you down the Fantô-mas express?"

"But I'll pull off his mask while he's coming, and if I don't like Fantômas, I'll pluck out his eyes . . . Isaac, I'm not a flirt. I've installed double locks on the terrace windows, and a whole new set of alarms. But couldn't you be my Fantômas, or are you still faithful to that Russian bitch?"

"She's Romanian," Isaac said. His darling was a double agent who'd disappeared from Gracie Mansion. Isaac had swindled her away from the FBI, and one afternoon Margaret Tolstoy kissed him on the mouth and ran from Isaac. She'd been gone six months, and all his probing, all the pressure a mayor could bear, couldn't bring her back.

"Isaac, you're safe. I won't seduce you."

Clarice hugged the mayor, ground her chest against his, and Isaac couldn't deny the electrical pull of his own flesh. He would have been attracted to Clarice in another world. But she was Marianna's mom, and touching Clarice would have been like courting incest.

He got his Glock back from Milton and Sam, and had his own man whisk him up to the Bronx, where he hoped to relax among the debris and forget about Fantômas. Jerome Avenue had become a whore's roost. Drivers coming off the Cross Bronx Expressway could have their pick of girls who loitered under the

Jerome Avenue El. The girls would lead their johns into the courtyard of the Castle Motel, a huge brick box with no windows on its outer wall. The girls had their own godmother, Mimi Brothers, a Bronx nurse who operated a van near the motel, distributing free condoms, flu shots, vitamins, sex education booklets, coffee, sandwiches, and chocolate bars. Mimi Brothers had the words "Heart of Gold" tattooed on her left bicep and kept a baseball bat inside the van. If some crazy client attacked a girl under the El, Mimi would come running.

Isaac shared a chocolate bar with her.

"Mimi, I promise you, one of these days I'll bring an ax and demolish that fucking motel."

"Isaac, you're a baby. That's why I voted for you. Demolition won't work. There'll always be a Castle Motel. At least if a girl shoots up, I know where to find her."

The godmother was short of cash, and Isaac contributed a hundred dollars to her kitty. Then he strolled up Featherbed Lane without his bodyguard. It had once been the most elite address in the West Bronx. Now it was a garden of broken bricks beside Robert Moses' expressway. He cursed that master builder, cursed him in his grave. But the mayor noticed something while he ranted: a painting on a wall. It wasn't the tropical landscape of some young Latino artist, or a fanciful dream of brotherhood that would never happen in the Bronx. It was an illustrated tombstone on a dead brick wall. There was the face of a fallen gang member with a little message, "Rest in Peace, Homey," and a detailed drawing of Featherbed Lane, with cars, prostitutes, and Moses' highway, like a grim paradise looming over the planet. The artist signed the obit in one corner with a large *A.*

Isaac kept walking. He found another obit by the same artist, another illustrated tombstone, with a harsh domestic scene of the Bronx: drug dealers and policemen in a *danse macabre.*

The obits disturbed Isaac and exhilarated him. Those young gang members who'd died in the Bronx had found their own chronicler in "A," who didn't draw fields of angels and demons, or metaphysical forests, just the psychic weather of Featherbed Lane.

Isaac ran down the hill, almost as excited as the first time he saw Anastasia, aka Margaret Tolstoy. He wanted to tell all his deputies about the artist he'd discovered in the ruins, right next door to the highway that had killed the Bronx.

3

The Bronx had its own historian, Abner Gumm. Isaac was dying to meet the man who'd photographed wild dogs in Crotona Park, torn curtains at the Paradise (one of the last movie palaces), shellshocked faces of young prisoners at a Bronx jail for juveniles. He'd spent fifty years in the street with the same simple box camera. Gumm received no salary as borough historian. He lived on a small inheritance.

The mayor invited him to lunch at the mansion. He was in his late fifties, like Sidel. He wore secondhand clothes, same as Isaac, who could feel Gumm's distress among the chandeliers and antique sofas. The borough historian was a slightly dysfunctional hermit who would have been hospitalized if he hadn't found a way to step back into the world with his box camera. Isaac was immensely fond of him after five minutes. He almost felt like asking Gumm to move into the mansion.

"*A*," Isaac said, with a toothpick in his jaw. "Tell me about that fucking genius. Give me a hint."

The borough historian began to blink.

"Come on," Isaac insisted. "We're street kids . . . we walk the line. You must have photographed those murals. They're unforgettable."

Isaac and Abner began to drink Harvey's cold potato soup. Both of them were wearing napkins pinned to their chest . . . in case they spilled the soup. It was clever of Isaac to have a cook who was also a valet. Harvey could feed the mayor and his guests and clean them up.

"Murals?" Abner had to ask.

"The ones on Featherbed Lane . . . to honor the locals who died in the neighborhood."

"Your Honor, I shot a whole series on Featherbed Lane less than a year ago. There weren't any murals."

"That's weird. They just bloomed . . . like cherry trees?"

"No. The gangs are inventive. I can't keep up with them."

"Like the Phantom Fives?"

"Featherbed Lane belongs to the Latin Jokers. I ought to know. I have a little card that lets me shoot in their territories."

"And if you didn't have a card?"

"I'd lose my camera . . . and my life."

"But I walked Featherbed Lane, and nothing happened. I didn't meet one Joker."

"They were there, Your Honor, but they avoided

you. You're a celebrity. They follow your exploits on the tube. They call you El Caballo, the Big Jew."

"Grand," Isaac said.

"You ought to be flattered. They're not usually that affectionate about a mayor. Manhattan's a forbidden planet to them."

"But I'm also mayor of the Bronx."

"In theory, yes. But your mansion isn't in Van Cortlandt Park. And you never had a power breakfast inside the Bronx Zoo."

"I hate power breakfasts," Isaac said.

"But you have them all the time."

"That's one of the liabilities of my office. Power breakfasts and power lunches."

"And they can't find much Manhattan treasure flowing into the Bronx."

"Jesus, I do what I can. We're in the middle of a baseball war, and it's the governor who controls the purse, not me."

"Billy the Kid means nothing to them. They're only interested in El Caballo."

"And I'm interested in an artist who's still unknown to my borough historian."

"I'm not God, Your Honor, but I'll shoot Featherbed Lane again."

Abner turned gloomy, wouldn't taste his dessert. Isaac had the rotten habit of always expecting too much from his soldiers. Abner Gumm had narrowed the arc of his interest to a borough that was like a bitter Manhattan suburb, some kind of kindergarten, and he'd covered that kindergarten as much as he could. But he couldn't catalogue every little Rembrandt.

"I'm sorry," Isaac said. "I didn't mean to pressure you. You're not an information bureau . . ."

The borough historian still wouldn't touch his dessert. He tried to unpin his napkin. He was only agile with his box camera. Harvey had to assist him.

"You can photograph the mansion if you like."

"I wouldn't know what to shoot . . . Manhattan isn't the right subject for me."

"But you're in the mayor's house."

"Forgive me, Your Honor, but it's like a glorified hotel . . . I'd only be shooting shadows."

And Gumm himself left like a ghost. Isaac was forlorn. He'd played the naif with Gumm. He knew all about the Latin Jokers. He'd recruited undercover cops from their ranks when he was a troubleshooter with the First Deputy's office. Isaac borrowed Fantômas' best lines of attack. He wore disguises out in the street, and for three months he ran a rival gang that nearly crippled the Jokers.

Later on, when Isaac himself was Commish, he had the Ivanhoes, who traveled where ordinary policemen weren't permitted to go. But he had to disband the Ivanhoes, and now he was left with one remote unit of outriders, the Bronx major crime brigade. He wasn't supposed to meddle in police matters, but Isaac was a born meddler. He often rode with Brock Richardson, the young assistant D.A. in charge of the brigade. And Isaac faxed him at his office in the Bronx County Building.

TO BROCK RICHARDSON, MAJOR CRIMES/BRONX
SUBJECT: MERLIN

MEET ME AT THE MANSION 1400 HOURS
(signed) SIDEL
P.S. I'LL CUT OFF YOUR BALLS IF YOU'RE LATE

Brock hadn't photographed Featherbed Lane. Brock wasn't the borough historian. But he slept in the same crib with the Latin Jokers . . .

Isaac heard someone hum in the kitchen. It didn't sound like Harvey or Mathilde or one of the maids. He strode into the kitchen with his Glock. Marianna Storm was ironing the mayor's shirts. She hovered over the ironing board with a tantalizing concentration. She had a watering can and Harvey's hundred-dollar iron. But Isaac couldn't locate any cookie batter. The oven was cold. He hungered for the smell of mocha chip . . .

"Marianna, Merliners don't have to iron, you know. That's not part of the agenda."

"Clarice cut off my allowance . . . you mentioned the hit man to her, and Mom is mad as hell. It was supposed to be our secret."

"Some slob in a hood tries to throw Clarice off her terrace, and I can't interrogate her?"

"He wasn't a slob," Marianna said.

"Are you in love with him too?"

"Love? Clarice has the hots for him, that's all."

"Don't talk like that," Isaac said. "You're twelve years old."

"And I'm ironing your shirts, Mr. Mayor. It will cost you twenty bucks an hour."

"That's robbery," Isaac said. "Harvey does my ironing."

"I'm glad. The City pays him, and you'll pay me."

"But you saw the hitter yourself. Tell me about him."

"Fantômas? He was polite . . . and his voice was familiar. I'm sure I met him somewhere without his mask."

"Then think," Isaac said. "I'll give you your wages, Marianna, but start to guess."

"I'll remember . . . when I hear his voice again."

"That isn't good enough. Guess!"

A man in cowboy boots came into the kitchen. He wore a denim shirt and a Glock under his belt, like the other members of the Bronx brigade. "Boss, have you been looking for me?"

Isaac ignored him. "Marianna, do you recognize that voice? Is he your Fantômas?"

"Don't be ridiculous," Marianna said. "You couldn't have Merlin without Mr. Richardson."

"Hey," Brock said, "what the hell is going on?"

Marianna ordered both of them out of the kitchen. "Will you let a girl iron in peace? I'm only human. I could set a couple of sleeves on fire."

Isaac moved onto the back porch with Brock. They sat down in rocking chairs, with their feet against the rails. Richardson was a pothead, but he wouldn't toke up in front of Isaac, and he always seemed a little deprived without his stash. One of his hands started to shake.

"Jesus," Isaac said, "you'll be incoherent in another five minutes if you don't light up."

"I'm fine," Brock said.

"I need you to find a kid. He does wall drawings. I caught two of them on Featherbed Lane, one near Macombs Road and the other near the El. He signs his art with an *A*."

Richardson's hands stopped shaking. He smiled at Isaac, breathed in imaginary smoke as if he were sitting on a mountain of Tijuana Red. "Boss, you don't have to worry. I can lead you right to the little man. His name is Alyosha . . ."

4

Abner Gumm walked across the "moat," an iron bridge that led into the Castle Motel. No one mistook him for a john. The boy who was guarding the gate, a fifteen-year-old Latin Joker with a Nighthawk, a machine pistol made of fiberglass, winked at the borough historian. "Hiya, Shooter."

"Mind the store," Abner said. "And stop peeking under the girls' brassieres."

"Shooter, they don't wear no brassieres."

"Then close your eyes, Abdul."

"How'm I gonna guard the store?"

"With the eyes in your ass."

A small band of prostitutes waited behind the moat for their afternoon fix. The Shooter had to supply them with drugs, or they were worthless inside the motel and out on the street. He'd hired a nurse, Mimi Brothers, to watch over them. He bought her a van, stationed her under the El, where she could feed them candy and spot the police or a Dominican gang that wanted to rip off the motel.

The Bronx historian had been in and out of psychiatric wards, a manic depressive who would drink his own urine and lick the paint off a wall. He couldn't have held a job. His mom and dad, who'd bought into a frozen yogurt franchise, had left him a series of annuities that matured like tiny explosions every five years. He lived off these "explosions," wandered the Bronx, photographed back gardens, buildings, and walls, searching for some unbelievably bald texture that could unlock his own barren music, and when this music became too hard to bear, he'd arrive with a suitcase at one of the wards, sit with Mimi Brothers, a psychiatric nurse who would give sponge baths to patients like himself. Mimi encouraged him to become a small businessman. He borrowed money, opened several motels under the Cross Bronx Expressway. He had little desire for scenic routes; he preferred brick and concrete along a brutal line . . .

The Shooter had prospered with the help of certain gangs, had discovered early on that he couldn't survive without them. He was loyal to the Latin Jokers, who stole all kinds of trees and plants and artificial grass for the motel's inner mall, which was now Gumm's secret garden. He'd built the motel like a bunker. Inside the outer bricks was a group of concrete bungalows, each with five or six bedrooms, a garage, and windows that could have been cannon emplacements. A john was perfectly safe within these walls. And so was the Shooter.

He had immediate police protection. Bernardo Dublin, a Bronx detective who'd come right out of the Jokers, lived at the motel. It wasn't the address Bernardo gave to the NYPD, but he kept all his clothes and guns with the Shooter. He had red hair and a red mustache and looked like an Irish-Latino linebacker. Sidel had plucked him off the streets, educated Bernardo, pushed him through the Police Academy. Bernardo owned a small chunk of the motel, had become a silent partner in most of the Shooter's enterprises.

He befriended the prostitutes, took his meals with them at the motel, lent them money, punched out any john who abused them or tried to set one of the girls on fire. He was like a hulking housemother with a gold shield and a Glock. Gumm found him writhing on the floor in the main room of the bungalow he and Bernardo shared. Bernardo wasn't wearing any clothes. He was drinking Polish vodka. His eyes were bloodshot. The red fur on his body resembled raw silk.

"Bernardo, guess who took me to lunch?"

"Father Time."

"Almost," Abner said. "El Caballo. He's fallen in love with Angel Carpenteros."

Bernardo's mustache began to quiver. "How did that happen?"

"Like it always does with El Caballo. He was stumbling around on Jerome Avenue. Mimi spotted him, or he might have walked into the motel. He took a hike on Featherbed Lane and saw Angel's art. He flipped over it, and got in touch with the borough historian. Me."

"What's the problem, Shooter?"

"If El Caballo gets himself a prodigy, he'll be poking around here all the time. You'll lose your crib, I'll lose mine . . . Bernardo, he'll close us down, crib after crib."

"So what? You'll open new ones. He's the mayor. His mind is blown out. He has the attention span of an ape . . . did you lie to him about Angel? The Big Guy is still good at catching lies."

"He'll never find Angel . . . because you're gonna ice the kid."

"Paulito's baby brother? You're dreaming, Shooter."

"Paulito's in isolation. And we'll keep him there. He'll never even notice the kid is gone."

"I'll notice . . . he's practically my godson." Bernardo crawled around with his rump in the air, dove under a table, retrieved his holster, and handed it to Gumm. "You kill Angel if you're so hot about it."

Gumm dangled the holster as if he were clutching a dead rat by the tail. "Me? I'm not mechanical. I wouldn't even know how to pull the trigger."

"You're handy with a camera, aint you?"

"It's nothing," Gumm said. "A simple box with a shutter. I solved it when I was five years old . . . but I still can't change the film."

"Then quit that prince of darkness routine. I'm not doing the kid."

Gumm's two-way radio began to whistle. "Shooter, Shooter, can you read?"

"Mimi, are you dropping pellets all over the place? Tone down."

"A pair of patrolmen just cuffed Daisy Pell."

"Where are they from?"

"Fox Street. The Four-One."

"What are they doin' so far afield?"

"We're getting famous . . . come on, they're walking her across the moat."

"Relax. Bernardo will handle it. Tell Abdul to hide his Nighthawk."

Bernardo took his holster back from Gumm. He'd already crept into his clothes. He was wearing jeans and a denim shirt from the Gap. He put on a mustard-colored jacket and cowboy boots from Buffalo Chips, and shot across the lawn to the registration office, where he met two beefy patrolmen who had Daisy Pell with her hands cuffed behind her back and were screaming at the Shooter's day clerk.

"We're gonna close you down, boy. Who's the hotshot around here?"

"I am," Bernardo said, rage building under his red mustache as he saw the handcuffs bite into Daisy's wrists.

"Well, son, we caught this young lady leading a john toward the premises."

"Where's the john?"

The patrolmen looked at each other, shrugged. "Who the fuck do you think you are?"

"Mr. Death . . . unshackle Daisy. The cuffs are too tight."

"And how much you gonna give us to uncuff the little sweetheart?"

"I'll give you your life," Bernardo said, pulling out his Glock and digging it between the first patrolman's eyes. The second patrolman fumbled with his keys and unlocked the handcuffs. Daisy Pell kissed Bernardo on the cheek and walked out of the office.

"Call your station," Bernardo said.

"What?"

"Call your station. Get your commander on the phone. I'd like to ask him why two clowns from Fox Street decided to rip off the Castle Motel. Did he put you up to this?"

"No. We just . . ."

Bernardo placed his gold shield against the second patrolman's mouth and made him kiss the metal.

"I'm with the anti-gang brigade, Detective Bernardo Dublin. Should I write down my shield number?"

"No, Detective. That isn't . . ."

"We've been staking out this motel for months, and when assholes like you interfere with our work, start making false arrests and asking a little key money, we have to discourage that sort of thing . . . get down on your knees. Both of you."

"Why?"

Bernardo kicked the first patrolman in the groin. Both of them got down on their knees, hugged the floor, avoided Bernardo's eyes.

"Who am I?"

"Mr. Death . . . Bernardo Dublin."

"You remember that."

Bernardo drove the two patrolmen into the wall with a barrage of punches and kicks. The Shooter leapt into the office and pleaded for the two patrolmen.

"Bernardo, you're killing them. We don't need that complication."

"They didn't have to hurt Daisy, cuff her so hard."

"She'll get over it," the Shooter said.

Bernardo stepped out onto the phony grass that reminded him of an archery range without archers. He thought of Angel Carpenteros, that kid the Shooter wanted him to ice, and he wondered how Angel would have drawn the Castle Motel. With archers perhaps and long, slender arrows that could pierce the armor of women, trees, and men.

Part Two

5

ROOSTER RAMIREZ OF FEATHERBED LANE

REST IN PEACE, HOMEY

PAID FOR BY THE LATIN JOKERS

Rooster had red hair. You couldn't see much of his eyes in the mural. But he wore a blue handkerchief on his head, with four little knots that represented royalty; he'd been one of the Jokers' wise men. Rooster was thirteen when he died. And it took Angel a whole hour to draw that handkerchief with the knots and get it to look like a crown.

Angel never liked to work from photographs. He had to know a face by heart. But he would spend hours picking through the family album of a dead boy, memorizing whatever he could. He was like a scavenger, but it was part of his profession. For all the dead homeys of the South Bronx, Angel was the only artist in town. He painted monuments on a wall. When a homey fell, hit by the cops or some motherjumper, the homey's gang would hire Angel to prepare a war memorial.

The Jokers would never haggle with him. Angel had the status of a priest. He prepared the little texts, decided on the drawing. The Jokers picked the wall, and Angel did the rest. His big brother, Paulito, who was in max security on Rikers Island, was the Jokers' mastermind. Paulito ran the gang from his prison cell. And it was because of Paul that Angel had acquired his monopoly on war memorials and could charge such an extravagant price. Rooster Ramirez, RIP, had cost the Jokers five hundred bills.

He was twelve years old and the richest kid in his class until he stopped going to school. He had a business to run and he had to nurse his bank accounts. Angel couldn't paint a wall after the sun went down. Light was precious to him, light was an unpredictable god. He couldn't piss it away inside a classroom, taking part in spelling bees and learning lies.

He was standing on his ladder, finishing Rooster's red hair, when he felt a chill on his back. He didn't have to turn around. He could smell Richardson's perfumed soap.

"You shouldn't come here," Angel said. "If the Jokers catch you, I'll lose my franchise."

Richardson laughed. "Who's been teaching you such big words, homey?"

He liked to wear suspenders and cowboy boots and carry a gun inside his pants. He wasn't a policeman, but he ran a whole brigade of cops whose only job was to break up gangs in the Bronx.

"You haven't been to see me, homey, and you haven't been to school."

"I'm an artist."

"Congratulations. But Picasso wasn't a hooky player."

"He would have been if he'd ever lived in the Bronx."

"Alyosha," Richardson said. Alyosha was some kind of a saint in a book called *The Brothers Karamazov*. And Alyosha was also a "saint" in Richardson's books at the county courthouse. Angel had tried to read *The Brothers Karamazov*, but he couldn't understand a line. A father kept biting his sons until the sons started biting back. They were all in love with a beautiful blond witch named Grushenka.

"I'm cutting loose," Angel said.

"Homey, you belong to us."

"I have a right to buy my soul back. I've been looking at law books in the library."

"Look again. You're on my payroll, Alyosha. And you're staying there."

"You've been corrupting minors," Angel said. "You could go to jail."

Richardson clutched Angel's pants and lifted him off the ladder. "And who could go right back into Spofford?"

Angel had spent three months at the Spofford Juvenile Detention Center when he was eleven; he had to punk for the older boys. Not even Paulito's reputation could reach inside a children's jail. The older boys had made him put on lipstick and wear a dress; he had to skulk around in high heels; one of the guards had fondled him. It was Richardson who got him out of there, and now he was Richardson's little man, a salaried stool pigeon of the Bronx brigade, who'd ratted on his own brother's gang.

"Put me down."

Richardson tossed Angel into his mustard-colored Ford. His men loved dark yellow; they had mustard-colored walls at their headquarters, mustard-colored notebooks, mustard-colored shoes.

"Richardson, lemme take my ladder."

"Leave it there," Richardson said and drove down Featherbed Lane. Angel wasn't worried. He was considered a holy boy in the 'hood. No one would touch his materials . . . or ask why that gangbuster, Brock Richardson, swiped him off the street; Richardson had declared war on the Latin Jokers, and it was only natural for him to kidnap Paulito's little brother, the Jokers' artist-priest.

He rolled a joint for Angel and himself. Richardson's brigade was full of dope fiends. You couldn't walk into his headquarters without the smell of grass. He called it medicine and mustard seeds. His hands were marked with that same mustard color. And he was turning Angel into an addict. The boy would lean back in that mustard-colored Ford and dream of getting out of the Bronx. He'd buy a condominium with the money he saved from his murals and sit in the dark until Paulito came home from Rikers. He couldn't really celebrate without Paul.

"Richardson, when's my brother getting out?"

"He's safe where he is . . . Paulito has his own fucking prison. He'd die out on the street. I'd have to kill him."

"He's only nineteen and his hair is turning white."

"So what? It makes him look distinguished. He's a gangleader, isn't he?"

"He's an old man," Angel said, his eyes burning from all the mustard-colored smoke. But even in his marijuana haze, he could tell that Richardson had cruised past the courthouse.

"Richardson, where the hell are we going?"

"To kindergarten."

"I thought you fixed it so I didn't have to go to school."

"It's a special kindergarten for little geniuses."

"Richardson, lemme out of the car."

Richardson was already getting crazy from the mustard seeds he'd sucked in. He pulled out his Glock and held it between Angel's eyes.

"I'll blow your fucking brains out."

"Richardson, you can't afford to glock me. I'm your little man."

Richardson shouldn't have been wearing a gun. But he was a prosecutor with his own brigade, an Indian fighter. And Angel had to laugh, because the Bronx's only Indians were wild kids like Rooster Ramirez, who were much more noble than anyone in Richardson's brigade.

All the Latin Jokers carried Glocks. It was a very temperamental gun. You could shoot yourself in the foot if you didn't carry it right. Angel couldn't remember who had started the habit. The Marines or the Mafia. But it had become the biggest status symbol in the Bronx. You could wear the wrong leather jacket, ride in the wrong car, but you had to have your Glock.

They drove across the Third Avenue Bridge, and Angel wasn't sure if he was in the mood for Manhattan. He had to finish raising up Rooster on a wall. Richardson rode into a park with its own guard at the gate. Then they got out and walked up to a mansion with white walls and a green door.

The house was full of people. They all looked like putas and cops and maricónes. Angel wanted to run. But Richardson blinked at him with his mustard eyes. "Behave yourself. You're my protégé . . . can you guess where we are?"

"Sure. It's the mansion of some hot millionaire who raises putas and maricónes."

"It's the mayor's house, little man."

Angel knew all about the Big Jew, Isaac Sidel, the first policeman ever to become mayor of New York. Angel had seen him on the tube with his sideburns and the dark eyes of a gypsy. The Big Jew could have come right out of Karamazov country. He was always crying at funerals and running around in the mayor's personal coach with a blanket on his knees, like Papa Karamazov. But he wasn't a miser or a moneygrubber. He wouldn't sit in the mansion and give himself to rich people. He wanted to remake the world. And now Angel understood what this little party was all about. Sidel had reached beyond the schools to start his own cultural enrichment crap. It was named after Merlin, the wizard of King Arthur's court. And all the maricónes were called Merliners. Angel would have to get the hell out of there. He wasn't going to join King Isaac's court. The Big Jew could toss him back into public school and that would bite into Angel's art career.

He darted past Richardson and got near the door, but a hand plucked him from behind and pulled him back into the crowd. "Maricón," he muttered, when he turned around and saw those telltale sideburns that belonged to Sidel, the guy who couldn't lose an election, who took the Bronx by storm, with ninety percent of the vote.

"Alyosha," the Big Jew said, and Angel was spooked, because Richardson had given out his code name. Isaac must have known that Angel Carpenteros, aka Alyosha, was the mascot and secret snitch of the Bronx brigade.

Richardson appeared behind him. "Brock," the mayor said, "thanks for bringing Alyosha. I've been waiting to meet the little moralist."

"Muralist, you mean," Richardson said.

"No, no," the mayor said. "He's a moralist . . . that's what moves me. His colors can condemn."

"Your Honor," Angel said, bolder now. "There's a bunch of children in the room. How'd you guess who I am?"

"It's your coat."

Angel was wearing his painter's rags. Richardson

— 43 —

hadn't given him a chance to change into street clothes.

"I asked Brock if he would invite you to join the Merliners . . . are you on his baseball team?"

"Mr. Mayor," Angel said, "I don't have much time for baseball."

Angel almost liked the Big Jew. The Jokers dressed much better than the mayor of New York, who was wearing a jacket that could have come out of a charity store. He looked like a brainy bum.

His deputies tore at his sleeves, and Isaac had to run off with them and solve ten riddles at a time, including a baseball strike that was beginning to sink the Bronx.

"Richardson," the boy said, "if the mayor knows who I am, I'll never leave this mansion alive."

"Angel, he lives in the clouds. He doesn't know shit."

"But you told him my name was Alyosha."

"So what? You sign your murals with a big fat *A*. The *A* could be anything. I'm building you up, little man. Alyosha sounds like an artist from the Bronx."

"But what if he peeks into your books and finds Alyosha."

"He can't peek. My books are confidential. But suppose he does. He'll think I stole that name from the real Alyosha. *You.*"

"I still don't like it. You can keep Merlin. I don't want to be enriched."

"It's too late. I scored my points with the Big Jew. I found Alyosha for him. I found the mural boy. I can't take him away. It would be suicide for me and my men. Isaac will kick us clear into the sea."

"But he'll learn that I'm a hooky player."

"Not a chance. He'll know what we want him to know. We're the warriors, you and me. He's just a king inside an enchanted cottage. Did you have a good look at him? His shoelaces weren't even tied. His socks don't match. He's like an ostrich with his head in the sand."

"I'm not . . ."

And then he saw a blond brat with blue eyes, a baby Grushenka, talking to King Isaac. Her bounciness and her beauty troubled Angel. She couldn't have come from the South Bronx. She took birdlike sips from her coffee cup. She had a paper napkin balled inside her sleeve.

"Who's that?"

"A Merliner," Richardson said.

Sidel brought her over. "Alyosha, meet Marianna Storm. She'll be one of your mates."

Marianna Storm cast her blue eyes on "Alyosha," and suddenly he was glad he had a code name.

"Alyosha is the most brilliant artist we have in the Bronx."

"Uncle Isaac, does he exhibit in one of the downtown galleries?"

Isaac ruffled his nose. "This kid doesn't do galleries. He paints on walls. It's strictly noncommercial. Alyosha remembers the dead."

And before Alyosha could take her telephone number, Richardson dragged him out of the mansion, making excuses to Isaac and Marianna Storm. "Isaac, the kid can't socialize too long. He's a month behind on his murals."

Angel began to sulk in Richardson's car.

"Why couldn't I do some exploring? The little puta likes me."

"Alyosha, you can rap all you want, strut like a rooster—"

"Don't say *rooster*. Rooster died because of us."

"Sorry. I'll be more careful. I'm lending you to the Merliners, but you can't get too close. You might start confiding in this Marianna Storm, and I'd lose my best little man. Play along with the Big Jew, kiss Marianna Storm in the dark, feel her titties, but you don't talk about yourself. Her father's the biggest honcho in baseball. J. Michael Storm."

"Never heard of him."

Richardson delivered Alyosha to the courthouse. They sat in the brigade's mustard-colored rooms looking at mug shots of every prominent gang member in the South Bronx. Half the borough was a no-man's-land. The cops couldn't rule the Bronx. They were like an invading army that would arrive during some explosion between the gangs. It was only Richardson's infiltration that could ruin a gang, Richardson's surgical strokes.

Alyosha sat behind three locked doors and spilled the foibles of Bronx bandits like Dog Face and David Six Fingers and El Rabbito, who would fall one by one, as Alyosha roamed among them like a little saint, pinpointing their activities.

"Rabbito is looking to whack David Six Fingers, because David slept with Rabbito's puta and has her underpants to prove it. I saw the panties. They're all red."

"And when's the massacre going to take place?"

"I'm not a mind reader, Richardson. But you ought to figure out where. At David's hobby shop on Jerome Avenue. Because David is crazy about model airplanes, and he lives on a steady diet of airplane glue. Now can I go home?"

"Not yet. What about the Jokers?"

"Richardson, they're asleep. They can't move without Paulito."

"That's not what I heard. They've been bopping around Hunts Point. And they've taken over a new housing project."

"What do you expect? You've been clipping so many gangs that the Jokers gotta fill the vacuum or some Dominican drugstore will move right into the project and start selling wholesale."

"Gimme the name of Paulito's new point man."

"My brother's not stupid. He picks a guy, and that guy gets socked in the head."

"Alyosha, who's walking point for Paul?"

"The Mouse."

"Mousy's a cripple, for Christ's sake."

"That's the whole idea. No one would expect a cripple."

"I don't believe it," Richardson said. "It's beneath your brother. Who put that stinking idea into his head?"

"Me. Alyosha."

Richardson stared at him. "Did Mousy ever do something to hurt you?"

"His cousin Felipe was at Spofford. And Felipe made me suck his dick."

"So Mousy has to suffer?"

"That's your choice, Richardson. But Mousy's holding the gang together. He's the Jokers' general. If you don't stop him, he's gonna win the Bronx."

"I can't go in and order a hit. It wouldn't be ethical."

"Get David Six Fingers to do it. He hates the Mouse."

"But David isn't on my payroll. I could get caught in the middle . . . hiring gangleaders to annihilate each other."

"Richardson, can I go home?"

"Not until you promise to talk to David. I'll give you a hundred extra bills."

"It's dangerous. A Joker can't walk into David's hobby shop."

"Come on, you're protected. You're a priest."

"David will get suspicious if I rat out my brother's new general. He'll throw airplane glue in my eyes."

Alyosha went down in the private elevator, reserved for judges, politicians, and registered rats. He arrived in the basement, which had once been a tiny jail and was now a canteen for court attendants and the district attorney's elite squad of cops, called the Apaches because they terrorized the Bronx. They were buccaneers who collected booty from whoever they could and stored it in the basement. They robbed from local merchants, from gangs like the Latin Jokers and the Phantom Fives, from druglords, from less ambitious pirate-cops who lacked the Apaches' organizational skills. Richardson's pool of men came from the Apaches. And *his* Apaches were so pernicious because a couple of them had graduated from the gangs themselves, had been recruited into the NYPD by Sidel himself, when he was with the First Deputy's office . . .

Alyosha walked through the Apaches' little warehouse and sneaked out the back door, landing opposite Yankee Stadium, with its great white bowl and its system of flags. Alyosha had never been inside that bowl. His uncles had told him about another stadium, a phantom field across the Harlem River, which once had a team of Latino All-Stars. Juan Marichal, Orlando Cepeda, the brothers Alou, who played like Apaches, eating up the National League. But that stadium had been destroyed, its hill taken up by a housing project. And Alyosha wondered what would happen to Yankee Stadium, which sat like another phantom field in the middle of a baseball strike. The Yankees had been keeping the Bronx alive. Now merchants were having heart attacks and feeding off the fat of their own lives.

Alyosha didn't care. He could draw his greatest mural on those phantom walls. He'd dedicate it to the brothers Alou. He'd paint every building in the South Bronx, even the ones that had been torched, call it Puerto Rican Paradise. But he had some business to do first.

He went into David Six Fingers' hobby shop on Jerome Avenue, right under the elevated tracks. David lived his whole life in the shadow of the tracks. He was thirty-three years old, war counselor of the Phantom Fives, which was a gang without real warriors. Paulito let the gang exist because he liked David, who had an extra thumb on his right hand and had sold Paulito model planes when Paulito was a little boy. David sniffed airplane glue all day and smoked hash in that dark closet of his. He had a pair of bodyguards, who were sitting on the floor playing Monopoly on a bumpy board, their Glocks sitting beside them. Alyosha could have glocked them with their own guns. But he'd have lost his status as a priest.

David Six Fingers sat in the gloom, holding a razor inside his extra thumb, carving a spacecraft that looked like a bullet with two heads. He was building a space station that would link the Bronx with Mars. He had all the concentration and the beauty of a boy. The modeling had saved him from the bitter rebellion of a ganglord. He modeled cars and planes with the swift imagination he used to plan attacks on an enemy gang. But the attacks failed. David's warriors didn't have the depths of David's mind. And the hobby shop was almost like a tomb. Children no longer came to buy his wares. David Six Fingers had to model for himself. But a hobby shop was made for children, and the lost revenue was killing David.

"Niño, I'm waiting for your brother to give me a license to sell."

"Paulito can't give out licenses. He's rotting away. The Apaches put him in max security and swallowed the key."

"And this isn't max security? A hobby shop without a hobby."

"Don't complain. Your troubles haven't started yet."

David Six Fingers slid the razor across his hand like a lizard. "Niño, I don't like pissy little painters threatening me."

"It's not a threat, David. Mousy's been getting big ideas. He's in love with your hobby shop. He wants it for the Jokers . . . as a canteen."

"Mouse wouldn't do shit without your brother's consent."

"I told you. Paul can't communicate. It's the Mouse's show."

"And what you want me to do? Beg the Mouse for some mercy?"

"No. Cut him with your razor, ear to ear. It's the only solution," Alyosha said.

"And why you telling me this?"

"Mousy's cousin made me suck his dick."

David blinked and dropped the razor. "Where? When?"

"At Spofford. And if the Mouse can't control his own cousin, he deserves to die. David, do what you want. Finish the Mouse or let him finish you."

Alyosha bought a Flying Tiger with some of the pocket money Richardson had given him, and David Six Fingers was stunned by the sale. The Flying Tiger had perfect markings. David had spent a month on the details, sanding and polishing every strut. He'd crawled into the womb of World War II, and he'd been modeling vintage planes like the Messerschmitt and the Fly-ing Tiger . . .

"You want me to wrap it in tissue paper?"

"No," Alyosha said. "I'll carry it home."

"It's delicate. The wind could . . ."

Alyosha walked out of the hobby shop, his fingers clutching the bow of the plane. He took a gypsy cab up to Mt. Eden Avenue and ran into the building where he'd lived with Paulito and now lived alone. He was the only tenant. The building had already been abandoned by its latest landlord. It had no electricity or running water. But Paulito had brought in a master plumber and electrician, who connected the pipes and the electrical outlets to the nursing home next door, and Alyosha had all his essential services. He even made monthly contributions to the nursing home. It was like paying his gas and electricity bill. And he didn't really mind being all alone. His mom had died of tuberculosis, and his pappy was running around somewhere, doing mischief. Alyosha was a child of the courts, but no court had come to claim him . . . after he got out of Spofford. He was supposed to be in the custody of Carmelita, his maiden aunt, but Carmelita had enough problems without him. A bastard son who beat her; a fiancé who robbed her blind. And Alyosha didn't like the neighborhood. Carmelita's only view was the Cross Bronx Expressway, a concrete ribbon that rose into the sky like a fat honeycomb filled with trucks and cars. He preferred the dead calm of Mt. Eden Avenue.

Alyosha went up to the roof with his Flying Tiger.

He could still smell the airplane glue under the paper wings. No one else on the planet could build a model plane like David Six Fingers. He wasn't born to lead a gang. But the Phantom Fives were the only homeys who had their headquarters in a hobby shop.

Alyosha launched the plane, let it glide over the roof, into the dark power of the wind, watched the paper begin to rip and reveal the wooden struts . . . until its skeleton was bared. Bits of David's best balsa wood fell away, and still the Flying Tiger flew, as indestructible as the Latin Jokers, and then a wing split, and the Tiger crashed into a wall of the nursing home.

6

Alyosha had to play the pious little priest when Mousy was found in a lot behind Featherbed Lane. His throat had been slashed, which was David's mark, but there were bruises under his eyes. He'd been punched silly before he died. And David didn't have the stamina to do that: his fingers were too fine. Alyosha didn't care whose mark it was. The Jokers commissioned him to paint Mousy on a wall. Alyosha stuck him next to Rooster. But he magnified the Mouse, multiplied him with his crayons and his brushes and his spray cans, drew him without much of a hump, because he wanted to give the Mouse all the perfection that befit a general. He worked half a day on the head alone, standing on his ladder like Michelangelo, his body half twisted so he could spray at the right angle.

But some downtown hunter descended on the boy and tried to swipe him off his ladder. "Richardson, will you cut it out, man?" Alyosha said, whirling his arms blindly, like a little windmill. "I'm not in the mood." But it wasn't that bloodsucker. It was a chauffeur in a Manhattan limousine. And this chauffeur was no ordinary hack. He was carrying a Glock inside his coat. Alyosha wondered if he was with the FBI, or was just a professional kidnapper working for a jailhouse gang that wanted to take revenge on Paulito and the Jokers.

"Fuck you," Alyosha said, "your sister has a dick."

The chauffeur made a fist, and then Alyosha saw Marianna Storm inside the limousine, and he said, "All right, hold your horses, grandpa. I'm coming down."

But the chauffeur wouldn't listen. He tossed Alyosha into the limo with Marianna Storm. "I hope you don't mind," she said. "I happened to be in the neighborhood, and Uncle Isaac asked me to collect you."

"Collect me for what?"

"The Merliners. We're meeting at my house."

"And you were out sightseeing on Featherbed Lane with the big barracuda, huh?"

"Milton? He's my bodyguard. But he shouldn't have been rough with you, Mr. Alyosha." And she turned to the chauffeur and lashed at him. "Milton, say you're sorry . . . you shouldn't have been so rough."

"Sorry, little mom," the chauffeur mumbled.

"Not to me, you numbskull. To Mr. Alyosha."

The chauffeur reached around to clasp Alyosha's hand. "Sorry, sir."

"Well," Marianna said, "we don't have all day, Mr. Alyosha. Do you forgive him or not?"

"Why do you need a bodyguard?"

"That's a silly question," she said. "Look at me."

Alyosha saw a girl with long white stockings, a plaid skirt, and a silver medallion.

"My mom's rich," she said. "I'm eminently kidnappable."

"They why'd you come to Joker country?"

"Are you deaf, Mr. Alyosha?"

"I'm Angel Carpenteros. The cops call me Alyosha."

"And so does Uncle Isaac. I came to collect you and have a quick look at your art."

"You can't have a quick look," Alyosha said. "It's a war memorial."

"I know that," said Marianna Storm, sitting back in her seat and signaling to her bodyguard, who brought Alyosha out of the Bronx in six and a half minutes and down to where all the rich barracudas lived on Sutton Place South . . . and followed him and her up to a penthouse apartment, with a terrace that wrapped around Manhattan. Alyosha could see all the bridges and gashes in the water that looked like screaming lines. Paulito was right to grab as many coca dollars as he could. Coca was the one Manhattan melody. And Paulito's gang was getting slaughtered on the street because they couldn't move coca around all by themselves and control the traffic without Paul. Wild men, like the Dominoes of Fort Tryon Park, were swooping down into the Bronx with all their brujas and their Santo Domingo shit and selling stuff right inside the schoolyards and making a fast million with all the lowlife peddlers, their little Dixie Cups. There was no point glocking a Dixie Cup, because new ones would jump out of the same box. And Alyosha was disheartened as hell until he saw the Big Jew munching potato chips inside the penthouse.

All the Merliners assembled around him, uptown and downtown kids he was bringing together for his own Manhattan melody. And with him was his prize, Bernardo Dublin, who'd been one of the Jokers' wise men . . . until he fell into Isaac's arms. Bernardo was a half-breed, with an Irish dad, and the Irish had adopted him at Police Plaza. He was with Richardson right now, with all the other Apaches. It was Bernardo who'd glocked Rooster Ramirez with the Rooster's own gun, caught him in the middle of a robbery, and pretended to be the angel of death. Alyosha hated Bernardo and owed him a lot. Because it wasn't Richardson himself who'd gone into Spofford and got him out. Bernardo had swept through that children's jail, battled with the guards, and grabbed Alyosha away from the warden without a writ.

Bernardo Dublin was six feet tall, with red hair like the late Rooster Ramirez and a slightly darker mustache. He had the dimples of a choirboy. Sidel paraded him to all his subjects.

"I had my religion," Bernardo said. "The king boxed my ears back."

"Never laid a finger on you," Isaac said, his mouth full of potato chips. "And I'm hardly a king, Bernardo."

"Boxed my ears with words. The mayor taught me how to read."

"That's a lie. Encouraged you is all I ever did. And I didn't have a mansion then. I was a policeman, wading in the muck . . . I'm not here to celebrate Bernardo, but to learn from him. We all can learn from Bernardo Dublin."

"Don't listen to Isaac. I'm a ruffian out on the street. I work with young gangleaders. I reason with them, the way Isaac reasoned with me. I'm like a preacher." Marianna Storm was already half in love with him, but the dimples and the red hair couldn't fool Alyosha. Bernardo Dublin was a snake. It was Bernardo who did the Mouse, punched him, cut his throat, like a copycat. He stole from David Six Fingers, took David's signature. He was always hiding behind somebody else's mark.

"I'm a convert," Bernardo said, with the Merliners hovering close. "I couldn't have gotten anywhere if Isaac hadn't given me a reading list . . ."

Alyosha broke away from the Merliners, sneaked downstairs, but there weren't any gypsy cabs on Sutton Place South. He had to hike up to Harlem before he could find anyone who'd take him across the river into the Bronx.

Marianna couldn't make much sense of it. But a word kept galloping inside her head, *Fantômas, Fantômas,* as if Fantômas were a pony she was riding. She had a pony, Lord Charles, at her grandpappy's ranch. But she imagined this horse in a mask. She blushed, because Bernardo was watching her. She liked him . . . and Alyosha, the boy who wanted to disappear inside his art. The painting had frightened her, because it revealed a rawness that could have rushed out of Marianna herself. Alyosha's colors were like the different temperatures of a bleeding sun. And Bernardo was part of the colors. He could have walked out of Alyosha's wall.

But she would never have imagined Bernardo in a mask. And then Clarice stumbled home from one of her parties . . . and fell into Bernardo's arms.

"Bernardo, be a dear, and get me a drink."

"We don't have alcoholic beverages," Bernardo said. "This is a children's reunion, Mrs. Storm. But I can make you a wicked Shirley Temple."

"No Shirley Temples," Clarice said. "Why don't you raid the freezer? There's a lovely bottle of Polish vodka."

"But you'll break Isaac's heart, introducing alcohol, ma'am. What if all the Merliners got drunk?"

"Then we'd have a wicked, wicked time."

"And Isaac would spank the both of us."

"That'd be sexy, wouldn't it, Mr. Bernardo Dublin?"

And Marianna didn't have to play Nancy Drew, girl detective. She could *feel* Bernardo's eyes under a hood, and it worried her, because Clarice must have felt them too. He wore that hood to hide his mustache and the red hair. But he had the swagger and the finesse of Fantômas. He held Clarice, steadied her, as if he were about to spin a prize top. And Marianna just couldn't believe that Bernardo Dublin, counselor to the Merliners, would have crept into Clarice's bedroom to toss her over the penthouse wall.

7

Alyosha didn't run back to his mural. The Mouse could wait. He went directly to David. There were no Phantom Fives on guard outside the hobby shop, and Alyosha couldn't see what was moving outside, because there was a big black curtain over the window, like a mourner's shroud. He made a wish that David was still alive. He didn't want to do David. No bruja had to tell him that drawing six fingers on a wall would bring bad luck. He liked David. He'd miss the model planes and the razor David kept inside his extra thumb.

Alyosha knocked on the glass. "David, it's me. Angel Carpenteros."

He saw a pull in the curtain. An eye appeared, like an octopus, and blinked. Then there was a crack in the door, and Alyosha had to enter sideways, or he'd never have gotten in. The hobby shop was all in a shamble. The struts of different planes were lying on the floor, like a mad assembly of wings. There were hundreds of chess pieces around, half of them guillotined. Someone had hacked off the heads of all the white horses, bishops, queens, and kings . . .

"I'm an orphan," David said. "My last two soldiers deserted me."

"Wha' happened?"

"Wha' you think? While I was out, the Jokers left me their calling card. I swear on my mother, I never touched the Mouse."

"It wasn't the Jokers, David. They wouldn't chop up your pieces like that. Chess is sacred to the gang . . . it was Bernardo. He did the Mouse. It's an old Apache trick. He gets rid of the Jokers, he gets rid of you, so he can sell our neighborhood to the Dominoes."

"Bernardo would give our fucking 'hood away to mad-dog Dominicans?"

"What does he care as long as he gets his cut? He protects the Dominoes and their Dixie Cups, gives them a fucking license, and he cleans up."

"I'll kill him," David said, the razor flicking inside his thumb.

"It's out of the question, David. That's what he's expecting you to do. Come after him, so he can glock you and get a fucking medal from the city. But if the Jokers don't grab you, David, he's gonna go for you himself. I could see it in his eyes."

"Then you're a bruja."

"No," Alyosha said. "I'm not a bruja. But I can read Bernardo. You'd better hide."

"Where, man? Should I go to Miami and peddle

snow cones to the Cubans? Or visit Frank Sinatra in Palm Springs? I was born under the El. It's home. I hate it outside the Bronx."

"Then lock your door and prepare a couple of hundred darts. Because the Apaches are coming."

"Wha' you gonna do?"

Alyosha ran to one of the witches who lived in a cellar on Burnside Avenue. She had a pimple on her nose and warts everywhere else. A bruja had to have a lot of blemishes, or she couldn't be trusted. Alyosha lit a red candle with her. You couldn't give a bruja orders, or ask her anything. You could only use her as a message board. Alyosha handed her fifty bucks and made a wish . . . that Bernardo would turn into a blind man.

But he must have been wishing out loud. The bruja rubbed her pimple. "Angelito, for five hundred dollars I can have Bernardo fixed."

Alyosha took back his fifty. "You're a bruja," he said. "You can't go into business."

He got out of there before she could boomerang that blindness onto him. He took a gypsy cab to Queens and crossed over the Rikers Island Bridge. They stopped him at the control booth.

"I have to see my brother," he said. "Paulito Carpenteros . . . he's in the max security center."

"What do we have here?" the guard said from inside his booth. "A little Latin Joker. Well, your brother's busy sucking dicks. He can't see you."

"That's a lie," Alyosha said.

The guard laughed, made a phone call from his booth, and let Alyosha onto the island, a fucking Monopoly board of jailhouses built in funny shapes, like beetles with their legs in the air. Paulito's building had thirteen legs at least. The guards were like high-tech clowns. They had crotch protectors and helmets with long plastic hoods. They prodded Alyosha with their riot clubs and delivered him to a conference room, where Paulito was waiting behind a grille. He was nineteen and could have been a hundred. He was wearing a silver cross with pure blue beads and the Jokers' knotted blue handkerchief hat. His hands had little cuts in them. His white hair had started to yellow.

"I hope it's important, Angel. I'll get twenty beatings for this visit."

"Bernardo's gonna wipe out David Six Fingers . . . and there won't be one hobby shop left in the Bronx."

"Your homeys are dying, and you worry about David Six Fingers?"

"Paulito, you loved his model planes, you always said so."

"Fuck his planes."

"But Bernardo's a rat bastard. He helped start the Jokers. He was a wise man once."

"Stupidhead, he's still one of us."

"But he's a cop . . . and the Dominoes are coming in . . . and David's gonna catch the shit. How can Bernardo be one of us? He'll collect dollars off every Dixie Cup."

"And so will we."

"But the Dixie Cups will sell in the schoolyards . . . to eight-year-old kids."

"And how can I deal with the crisis, huh?"

"You own the neighborhood, Paul."

"I lent it to Bernardo while I'm in the graveyard. The Dixie Cups won't go near a fucking school."

"And who's gonna police them?"

"Bernardo."

"The Apaches don't care about kids."

Paulito walked away from the grille, and Alyosha got out of there before the guards could pick his pockets.

He had a guest when he got home. The great Bernardo had picked all the locks and helped himself to a cup of coffee. He was standing in his mustard-colored holster, like the king of Mt. Eden Avenue. But he wasn't smiling. He had a twitch in his dark red mustache. He sipped his coffee, turned, and punched Alyosha in the face. Alyosha sat on the floor with a bloody mouth while the Apache kicked him like a dog.

"You went to a bruja and asked her to blind me."

"You can't ask a bruja anything," the boy said, catching his breath between Bernardo's kicks. "I only made a wish."

"And you wished me blind and dead."

"It don't matter, Bernardo. Brujas never listen."

"She listened . . . you little cocksucker, didn't I risk my gold shield to get you out of Spofford? I had to kick ten counselors in the ass."

"Don't call me *cocksucker.*"

"What should I call you? Weren't you wearing lipstick when I found you?"

"Mousy's cousin made me wear it."

"And what happened to the Mouse? He's on your mural list."

"Thanks to you, Bernardo. You grabbed him and cut his throat, so it would look like David did it."

All Alyosha could see was red hair and little brown eyes as Bernardo began to kick him without mercy. "I'm a murderer, huh? Say it again. Who carved the Mouse?"

Alyosha had to curl up and collapse himself like a telescope to kill the pain. "I don't know, Bernardo. I made a mistake."

The kicking stopped. Bernardo leaned over him in his mustard-colored boots. "Angel, I didn't mean to hit you so hard." He took out his handkerchief and wiped the blood off Alyosha's mouth. Then he picked him up, sat Alyosha down in a chair, and gave him a cup of coffee from Alyosha's own espresso bar. "You shouldn't have run out on the mayor. He only started Merlin because of little cocksuckers like you."

"Well, I don't need cultural enrichment," Alyosha said, with strings of blood in his coffee cup.

"You ought to be grateful that the Big Guy is interested in you. He picked me right out of the Jokers. I shouldn't be a cop. It isn't legal. But Isaac got rid of my rap sheet. He made my whole fucking record disappear."

"He's Merlin the magician."

"Shaddap. He gave me the gift. I was a fucking illiterate cocaine sucker until the Big Guy turned me around. He taught me how to live. Have you ever been to Chantilly, France? Have you ever crossed the moat to the little castle and seen the painting of the woman with the snake around her neck? Well, I did."

"There are plenty of snake women in the Bronx."

"Shaddap. I've been to Europe and Hawaii. Where have you ever been?"

"Nowhere, Bernardo. The only moat I ever crossed was the Third Avenue Bridge."

"Shaddap. The Big Guy loves your murals. You ought to be glad."

"How do I get to Chantilly?"

"You're coming with me to David's museum. We're gonna sniff some airplane glue."

"Leave him alone. He can't harm you. He doesn't even have a gang."

"He's still a general. There won't be any Phantom Fives after I pull on David's chain. The gang dies with him."

Alyosha could see the logic grow out of Bernardo's red hair. "What's so important about the Phantom Fives?"

"Don't get stupid. The Dominoes are coming. And I have to give them guarantees."

"But their Dixie Cups will fall in love with David. They can fly David's planes while they're selling dope."

"Shaddap. David's out of the picture."

"I'm not gonna help you butcher him."

"Yes you will. I own your little ass. Paulito promised you to me . . . you think I got you out of Spofford because I like your looks?"

"Paulito shouldn't have promised . . . he's a fucking Apache."

Bernardo grabbed Alyosha's collar and lifted him right out of the chair. "You're nothin' without Paul. You wouldn't have your murals, you wouldn't have a coffee bean."

"I can paint without commissions from Paul."

"Shaddap. Your brother owns every wall in the Bronx. Remember that." He dropped Alyosha back into his chair. "Now finish your coffee."

They went down the hill to Jerome Avenue. Alyosha could already see the Dixie Cups working in the dark. The oldest of them wasn't even Alyosha's age. They were like cattle that you kicked around and could exchange for other cattle.

Alyosha didn't know what to do. How could he warn David Six Fingers with Bernardo sitting right on his tail? David must have been out of his mind. Or else he was playing the fox. Because he'd removed the black curtain from his window. And he'd dressed that window like Alyosha would dress a wall. Six Fingers had painted a sky in the background, with a beautiful red sun and not a single broken building.

Alyosha didn't have to ring the bell. David's door was open. All the lights were on: it was like a soft, glowing midnight inside the hobby shop. Alyosha saw Messerschmitts and Lockheed Lightnings and Spitfires hanging from the ceiling like blind chandeliers. David must have rebuilt his best model planes, because there weren't any struts lying on the floor.

Bernardo stood behind Alyosha and called out, "David, darling David, where the fuck are you?"

But he shouldn't have bothered to call. Alyosha nearly shit inside his pants. He felt like a bruja who could read David's midnight sun. He wasn't even startled when he saw one of David's shoes in the aisle. David Six Fingers was sitting in a chair next to his cashbox, with a razor inside his freak thumb. He'd slit his throat and sat there bleeding to death, with a smile on his face.

Alyosha couldn't even call it suicide. David Six Fingers had saved his fucking soul. Because it wasn't David that Bernardo had zipped inside a body bag and sent to the morgue. David had gone out of his body while he sat in his own blood and went into those blind chandeliers, the Messerschmitts and the Lightnings, which Alyosha plucked out of the air before Bernardo could say a word and carried home to Mt. Eden Avenue.

No one commissioned him to do a mural. The Phantom Fives were defunct. But Alyosha painted David on the wall outside his own building. He stood on his ladder and did Jerome Avenue, with the elevated tracks; the buildings all had one lit window, like a burning eye. And Alyosha painted a Messerschmitt over the tracks. David stood in the middle, and Alyosha drew the details of David's extra thumb. He didn't care if all the brujas and devils in the Bronx came after him. He couldn't do David without the thumb.

Dixie Cups began appearing under Alyosha's ladder.

They crossed themselves and squashed ten-dollar bills
into Alyosha's pants. The Dominoes arrived in a Cadillac, blew on their hands, blinked at the mural, and
rode away. And then Alyosha heard sobbing behind
him.

The Big Jew had come to the South Bronx. Sidel,
with his sideburns all white. He cried so hard that a
gun fell out of his pants and clattered on the pavement
with the dull, dead ring of a Glock. And Alyosha remembered now. It was Sidel who had started the
craze, who was the first policeman in New York to
have his own "designer gun." He'd brought the Glock
back from Austria after visiting the birthplace of some
bruja called Freud.

"Uncle Isaac," Alyosha said, taking liberties with the
Big Jew. "You shouldn't cry while I'm painting. It
brings bad luck."

"Sorry," Isaac said, blowing his nose with a mustard-
colored handkerchief the Apaches must have given
him. He watched while Alyosha did the lettering.

DAVID SIX FINGERS OF JEROME AVENUE

REST IN PEACE, GENERAL

PAID FOR BY THE PHANTOM FIVE RESCUE FUND

"He must have been a golden boy," Isaac said.
"He was a gangleader. He slit people's throats."
"I've done much worse than that," Isaac said.
"Your Honor, you don't have to confess."
"I'm not. I just wanted you to know where we

stood. The next meeting of Merlin will be at my house."

"I'm not so sure I'm coming," Alyosha said.

"I hope you will," the mayor said. "You're a Merliner, one of us."

And the Big Jew vanished in his car like the magician that he was.

"Merliners," Alyosha muttered to himself, Merliners, and went back to his mural.

Part Three

8

The baseball czar was rushing to Milwaukee. Isaac had to sit with him in Continental's first-class lounge at JFK. Isaac didn't have a first-class ticket, didn't have a ticket at all, and J. Michael had to sneak him into the lounge. He was a trespasser here, and J. Michael was enjoying himself. He ordered a preflight vegetarian meal. The hostess brought him chopsticks, and Isaac watched J. Michael eat grilled vegetables and guzzle three screwdrivers.

"J., give me one fucking sign of hope that I can bring back to my deputies."

"Why? The owners are already talking about phantom teams, with players they can pluck out of the bushes . . . like they did during World War Two. I'll have to punish them, Isaac. It's the only solution."

"J., I hope you drown in your own poisoned spit."

"Isaac, I'm a hero. The Democrats *and* the Republicans are putting out feelers."

"Feelers for what?"

"I'd make a terrific backstop in 'eighty-eight for either Party."

"With your past? They'll crucify you."

"Don't bet on it. Ex-radicals are the rage. Didn't Ronnie Reagan come crawling out of the far left? J. Michael Storm for vice-president, the man who fought the baseball owners tooth and nail, who wouldn't give in to monopolies."

"It won't wash. The players have their own monopoly . . ."

"Isaac, enjoy the sunshine, will you? The strike is bringing you prominence. Even Billy the Kid has been backing away from you."

"He knows I'll bite his face if he comes near me."

"That's not the reason, old son. I saw Seligman last month . . . from the Democratic National Committee. They are warming up to you, Isaac, a guy with your voter appeal. 'Vice-presidential timber,' that's what Seligman said. But not for 'eighty-eight. Can't have a pair of New Yorkers on the same ticket. It would scare the pants off the Southern boys, and kill our chances in the West. But you have a future, Mr. Mayor."

"The only future I want is an end to the strike."

"Then talk to the owners and start kicking ass. Because if they use phantom hitters and fielders, I will personally demolish baseball. And you can quote me on that."

"What about your own phantom fielder?"

"What the fuck does that mean?"

"Somebody tried to deck Clarice . . . and he was wearing a mask."

"You believe her fantasies, huh Isaac?"

"Marianna saw him too."

"And you think . . . ?"

"You're short of cash, and don't deny it."

"So I advertise for a man in a mask and send him after Clarice? Isaac, I don't have the money to enter that kind of league. Raskolnikov is aging a little. I have two mistresses I can't afford . . ."

"Why don't you punch me in the face? I accused you of plotting to murder Clarice."

"Because I'm not so innocent that I haven't considered it. But the strategies never seem to work. I didn't become the players' czar out of kindness. I'm a field general, a damn good one. I'd rather Clarice were dead. I'd have my daughter back . . ."

"I doubt it, J."

"Trust me. I'd woo her back. But if I'm gonna play backstop to Billy the Kid, I can't afford a murder in the family right now."

"You cold-blooded prick. I should have let you rot in jail . . . the great apostle to Uncle Ho."

"Isaac, have you ever read Uncle Ho? He was colder than I am . . . but beautiful. He said a single ribbon can destroy a whole chain of events. And I've been looking for that ribbon all my life."

J. Michael stood up, sucked on his screwdriver, and prepared to board his plane. Isaac was still confused about Fantômas.

He called Special Services on the ride back to Manhattan, tracked his son-in-law to a theatre on Broadway, had him paged after the first act, went across the street to a Greek diner where he could order a chopped salad with feta cheese and nurse a glass of pink wine with resin while he waited for Barbarossa.

Joe entered the diner looking like a dream in a hand-painted tie (Isaac's own daughter must have found the tie for Joe). He always wore black leather, like any homicide detective, until Marilyn started grooming him. Now he'd appear in powder blue and parrot green.

"Joey, is it Madonna tonight, or Michelle Pfeiffer?"

"Close. A princess from Surinam. She's fourteen."

"Great. We could kidnap her for the Merliners."

"Dad, I want my old squad . . . every cop I meet is scared shit of me. I'm worse than the plague. Isaac Sidel's son-in-law. I'll die without the street."

"You have Marilyn."

"Dad, we weren't discussing my wife."

"Joey, I didn't ground you, swear to God. Somebody thinks they're doing me a favor."

"Somebody like Sweets?"

Sweets had been Isaac's First Deputy and was now Commish. He wouldn't let Isaac near Police Plaza. But Isaac had obliged him to reassign Joe. Isaac didn't want his son-in-law running across roofs. Joe was Marilyn's tenth or eleventh husband, and Isaac couldn't bear to see her become a widow. Besides, he was really fond of Barbarossa.

"I have a little work for you, Joey."

"Dad, you initiating me into the Ivanhoes? Should I cross my heart and swear to uphold all your secrets?"

"I don't have secrets. I want you to follow a certain lady, dog her steps, go wherever she goes."

Barbarossa smiled. Isaac's son-in-law looked like Gable in *Gone With the Wind*, with little scars on his face and a white glove that hid a war wound from Vietnam.

"Dad, is it a new romance?"

"I'm engaged to Margaret Tolstoy."

"But she's missing."

"I'll get her back. This lady is the wife of J. Michael Storm."

"Your old student?"

"J. was never my student. I helped him stay out of jail. Somebody is trying to off his wife."

"And you think Storm is behind it?"

"I don't know. But the striker has a very strange MO. He wears a hood when he calls on Clarice . . . like Fantômas."

"And you expect me to find the bum? . . . I'd rather guard the princess from Surinam. Tell the lady to go to the police."

"You are the police."

"No I'm not. I'm Sidel's son-in-law, which means I have to wear a cape like Captain Marvel and jump into one of the mysteries you like to manufacture. Dad, leave it alone. You're not the Pink Commish anymore."

"Joey, Clarice has a child. I'm worried about her. I don't want this fucking Fantômas tiptoeing across her bedroom. He's a regular acrobat, climbing up walls . . .

do me a favor. Gimme Fantômas, and I'll get you back into the squad room. You can catch as many homicides as you want."

"Meanwhile I'm a floater . . . in the service of Sidel."

"One more thing. We won't tell the lady we're watching her. It's between you, me—"

"And Fantômas," Barbarossa said.

Isaac scribbled Clarice's address and handed Barbarossa a photograph he'd taken of her and Marianna at a meeting of the Merliners. Joe was startled: he could barely tell mother and daughter apart; they made a gorgeous attack team.

"They look like twins . . . Dad, Marilyn doesn't like it when you forget to show up for dinner."

"I'm the mayor. I have a million things on my mind."

"Like rinsing your mouth with retsina and dreaming of maniacs who climb up walls."

"Joey, I never dream . . . just help me out."

"Then don't disappoint Marilyn again . . . next Friday. Bring a date or a couple of your brats."

"I'll have to look at my agenda."

"Fuck your agenda, Dad."

He kissed Isaac on the forehead, walked out of the diner, and went back to his princess from Surinam.

9

Billy the Kid began to climb on Isaac's back. The governor demanded that the mayor meet with him. Isaac didn't respond. He was thinking of the hospitals that Billy the Kid wanted to close in the bitterest sections of Brooklyn and the Bronx. Billy had the bankers behind him. The hospitals were bleeding money. There were empty beds all over the place. But Isaac knew about the creative arithmetic that Billy liked to practice. The citizens of Brownsville and El Bronx could barely afford to live or die in hospitals that had been built for them. They could never get past the bureaucratic maze. And Isaac couldn't provide them with medical insurance. He wasn't that much of a magician.

He ducked Billy the Kid. He sat in his chopper, rode above the city, where he was safe. Isaac had a chopper at his command night and day. He did his best thinking in the sky, with his ass on a bucket seat, the wind beneath his collar, seagulls scattering above him, scared of the blades. He would land on the roofs of certain projects, watch the grim domain that was part of Isaac's own housing stock. He was the pharaoh here, the landlord of brittle, broken buildings that he would have loved to dynamite. And while he was on one particular roof, a pair of choppers swooped out of the sky. They were bigger than Isaac's, crowded with policemen in civilian suits. Isaac wondered if the Secret Service was already guarding Billy the Kid, who hadn't entered a single primary. Or perhaps the governor copied from Isaac, and had his own cadre of Ivanhoes. It didn't really matter. They were brutal men with glass guns, those Nighthawks that Dominican druglords favored. But these weren't Dominicans. They wore little radios plugged into their ears. They surrounded Isaac. He got out of his chopper and entered a bigger one, where Billy the Kid sat with a bear rug on his knees.

"Isaac, you shouldn't fuck with the future president of the United States."

"Win one primary before you start to brag."

"The primaries are a booby trap. I don't plan to self-destruct. I'll have all the delegates I need."

"A closed convention, huh Billy?"

"Not at all. After the candidates start knocking each other off, you'll have one lone eagle left. Billy the Kid."

"And who's going to introduce Billy the Kid, nominate him?"

"You. My law and order man. You'll dazzle the convention."

"Billy," Isaac said, clutching his own heart, "I'd rather go blind than nominate you for president. You're a murderer and a maniac."

"And who isn't?" said Billy the Kid, crinkling his blue eyes. He'd gotten rid of a black prostitute who might have compromised him and his election plans. He'd had men and women beaten up in order to erase the crooked lines of his past. He was capable of losing Sidel, pitching him into the ocean. Isaac was already seasick.

"Have your fun, Billy. But I'll tear your throat out the next time you kidnap me."

"Kidnap you, Sidel? Is that what you call a friendly chat over the skies of Brooklyn? . . . you'll play the good little kitten and nominate me. Because if you don't, your baseball war will never end."

"Ah, that's why J. Michael wasn't so eager to negotiate. You have him on a leash."

"A very short one. He'd love to be my vice-president."

"Billy, I wouldn't count too much on J. He was the meanest student radical I ever met. He's liable to topple you on the way to the White House."

"Let me worry about J. Michael . . . do you want the Bronx?"

"Yes."

"Then behave," Billy said. His eyes were killer blue. He signaled to his pilot, and Billy's chopper began to dance toward the housing project.

"And what if the strike goes on and on?" Isaac asked as the chopper bounced onto the same roof where Billy the Kid had found him.

"Then you're home free, Sidel. You can boycott the convention."

Isaac stared into the wind. Billy's chopper began to rise like a bewildered bumblebee.

"What about Margaret Tolstoy?" Isaac asked, but Billy could no longer hear him. Isaac continued to shout. "Do you know where she is?"

Billy the Kid waved to him, and Isaac returned to his own small chopper. He crossed into the Bronx, landed on a knoll in Claremont Park, climbed out, and picked up Alyosha, who was hiking on Featherbed Lane.

"Come with me."

Alyosha didn't complain. He followed El Caballo into Claremont Park, climbed into the chopper, and rode away from this ratland. He'd never sat in the middle of the sky, next to clouds that could have been candy. El Bronx looked like a long, curling plain, where even the rawest building had its own crooked geometry. He couldn't admit it to Uncle Isaac, but riding on a chopper over Paulito's territories was better than Disneyland, and he didn't even have to leave the Bronx. The chopper scraped its shadow on the roofs, like a dark, scratchy bird, but Isaac wouldn't let him lean over his bucket seat and follow each scratch.

They bumped along the Harlem River into that canyon town called Manhattan, and Alyosha didn't like it, because *his* geometry was lost among all the outcroppings of glass and steel and stone. He saw roofs and ceilings, but it was hard to find any floors . . . until the chopper plunked down into a narrow field next to the United Nations, where a limo was waiting for El

Caballo. But Isaac wouldn't get into a car. He dragged Alyosha up to Sutton Place South, barked at the doorman, and his favorite little Merliner, Marianna Storm, came floating out of the elevator with her silver medallion and long white socks. She smiled at Alyosha and let El Caballo kiss her hand.

"Hello, princess," Isaac said.

"Don't flatter. I'm not in the mood."

She laced her own arm in Alyosha's and they walked downtown with El Caballo beside them, people staring at her and the mayor. They climbed up a hill near Grand Central and arrived at a tiny village that looked like Featherbed Lane. It had its own garden and bicycle shop. Alyosha examined brick walls that would have been terrific for his murals.

"Your Honor, who lives here?"

"It's Tudor City," Isaac said.

"Yeah, yeah, but I'm not worried about names. Who lives here?"

"Doctors, dentists . . . and my daughter."

"And they're not about to hire me."

"Hire you for what?"

"To decorate their walls . . . don't they have a coupla dead sons and daughters here? Uncle, couldn't they use some war memorials?"

"I'll ask around," Isaac said.

The buildings looked like several of the castles Alyosha had seen in the Bronx, on Kingsbridge Terrace and Fort Independence Street, castles that were sixty years old, and must have housed rich people trying to escape the rot of Manhattan. Maybe Alyosha could find a castle somewhere for Paulito and himself. But he'd need a wider clientele than the Latin Jokers. Even if the Jokers dropped like flies, Alyosha could never get rich . . .

A chiquita with brown eyes and curly hair came to the door. She had a very slight mustache. Alyosha admired the way she stood with one hand on her hip. El Caballo's daughter, Marilyn the Wild. She'd married a cop who was as big a ballbuster as Bernardo Dublin. Joe Barbarossa, with a white glove on his hand.

The chiquita served lamb chops around a big table. He liked her aroma as she hovered next to him and speared a lamb chop into his plate. He sipped lemonade with Marianna, while Marilyn drank whiskey and wine with Isaac and the ballbuster, who was very polite and didn't wear his Glock to lunch. Marianna pinched Alyosha under the table.

"Don't you dare fall in love with Marilyn the Wild," Marianna whispered. "She already has a man, in case you didn't notice."

"I noticed," Alyosha whispered back. A sadness suddenly gripped him, because he couldn't even remember one family meal with his mom and pappy and Paulito. His mom started coughing blood into a napkin when he was a little kid and died coughing the same blood. It was Alyosha who had to prepare her meals while his pappy was out stealing television sets and Paulito was grabbing territory as the supreme general of the Jokers. Marilyn the Wild smelled like his mom, walked like his mom, with the same hippy motion.

Isaac sat down with Barbarossa after lunch and

Alyosha played gin rummy with Marianna and Marilyn the Wild. He tried not to listen to Isaac, but he couldn't help himself. He was a born spy, married to the Bronx brigade.

"Bernardo?" Isaac said. "I can't believe it."

"Dad, it's like his own private delicatessen . . . he comes and goes."

"But Clarice could have hired him to protect her from Fantômas."

"Yeah, and I could have a sex change and wear Madonna's tits . . . Dad, he's with her all the time. I tracked them to the Bronx zoo. They were humping in the fields, like grasshoppers."

"Shhh," Isaac said, rolling his eyes in Marianna's direction. But she wasn't a snoop, like Alyosha.

"You just don't want to piece it together, Dad. You don't want to see the whole cloth. I can't tell you why Bernardo was there with his mask. Somebody could have been paying him to frighten her. But bingo! He likes what he sees . . ."

"Joey, it doesn't hold. It wasn't the first time he met Clarice. He's with Merlin, for Christ's sake. I couldn't have started it without him."

"Dad, you're missing my point. It's only while he's Fantômas that he falls in love."

"Ah, you're a fucking romantic."

"I'm not, but Bernardo is. And Clarice falls in love with the mask."

"So he comes to hurt Clarice and climbs onto the mattress with her."

"But isn't that what Fantômas is all about? . . . danger and sex."

"Joey, don't lecture, please . . . I'm disappointed in Bernardo."

"Dad, don't your best pupils turn around and whack you in the head?"

"All the time," Isaac muttered, and the party was over. He collected Marianna and Alyosha and started to leave, but Marilyn cornered him.

"Did you enjoy the meal?"

"Delicious."

"Isaac, we hardly talked."

"We're too much alike to even bother. I look at you, and you look at me. It's better than talk."

"And we'll go on avoiding each other all our lives . . . dancing on different planets. Go on, get out of here, Mr. Mayor."

She kissed Alyosha and Marianna Storm, held them both in her arms, and nudged them out the door.

Isaac whisked them down the stone steps behind Tudor City and returned to that little heliport near the United Nations. El Caballo was taking Alyosha back into the sky, and baby Grushenka had decided to come along.

As the chopper climbed, Marianna closed her eyes and clung to her bucket seat. Isaac had already strapped her in. Every idle boy on Sutton Place South, between the age of twelve and twenty, tried to court Marianna, and she only cared about an artist from the Bronx who sketched dead people and liked to eat with his hands. She looked at Alyosha, but he was building clouds inside his head. That's what artists were like, she imagined. Always building clouds.

"Alyosha," she said, "can't you dream about anything but your drawings?"

It wasn't drawings that he was dreaming of. It was Bernardo the ballbuster. Alyosha didn't understand anything about masks. He saw that El Caballo was asleep, and he shouted in Marianna's ear, above the churning of the blades. "Who's Fantômas?"

"My mother's killer boyfriend," she shouted back. "He loves to wear a mask."

Alyosha was still confused, but he grabbed baby Grushenka by the hand. "Could I be *your* Fantômas?"

"Angel Carpenteros, you haven't even kissed me yet."

Alyosha reached as far as he could in his bucket seat and kissed Marianna on the mouth, while El Caballo snored and the chopper rode above the Third Avenue Bridge.

10

Bernardo never intended to have his own little court at the motel. But he couldn't shun the madres of Mt. Eden and Jerome, who stood outside his bungalow in the rain, without umbrellas or a shawl. The gate boy, Abdul, was terrified of them, because they looked like brujas with wet black hair. And when Bernardo arrived from his headquarters at Boro Hall and found their sad faces, he would invite them inside his bungalow for a cup of coffee and a dish of ice cream, lend them towels and his own hair dryer. Then he would ask, "Mothers, how can I help you?"

The madres would group around his leather chair and deliver their tales of woe. And these tales grew worse once the Dominoes "parachuted" into El Bronx. The parachuters and their Dixie Cups were selling drugs to niños in the neighborhood, bothering little girls, and had raped a retarded twelve-year-old in a schoolyard on Walton Avenue.

"Mothers, I would like to visit with the girl after you have finished your ice cream. She could tell me things about her attackers. I'm only a policeman. I need clues."

"She's in a coma, Don Bernardo . . . but we can tell you things, important things. The one who attacked her had a milky eye . . . and a blue mustache."

"A blue mustache," Bernardo repeated.

"Calls himself Panther."

"Mothers, I will do my best . . . you will have no more panthers in the Bronx."

He kissed all the madres, who blessed him and gave Bernardo their holy beads to protect him from Panther. Bernardo had another dish of ice cream, put all the beads into his coat pocket, left his Glock on the chair, and summoned Abdul, who was a half-breed, like Bernardo himself. Abdul had an Egyptian mom and a dad from Panama, but he was a city wolf, a child of the barrios, a kamikaze who seemed to survive any suicide mission.

"Say nothing," Bernardo said. "Do nothing. Just let the glass gun peek out of your coat. That's all the eloquence we need."

"Bernardo, who are we tracking?"

"A Domino with a blue mustache."

"That's bad. Panther never goes anywhere without an army."

"Then it's our rotten luck," Bernardo said.

They walked under the El to Shakespeare Avenue; Bernardo sang a few words inside a telephone booth, and a white Cadillac appeared. Bernardo entered the

Cadillac without Abdul. Martin Lima, one of the Dominoes' five ruling princes, sat on several cushions, with a pair of teen-aged girls in his lap. He had no bodyguards, only a driver with a Nighthawk cradled in his arms. The girls' eyes began to flutter. They were barely old enough to have breasts and were the prince's own personal crack babies, with brutal red lipstick . . . and Glocks strapped to their thighs. Bernardo felt like strangling Lima, but he couldn't interfere in a prince's sexual politics, particularly if the girls came from the Dominoes' harem in Washington Heights.

"Jefe," Bernardo said, "forgive me, but I have to ask. The niñas on your lap, are they local?"

"Dublin, I signed a treaty with you and the Jokers. I wouldn't touch niñas from the Bronx . . . but is that why you called me? You becoming a chicken inspector for the Jokers?"

Martin Lima was a fat boy with pockmarks on his face, a computer wizard from Fort Washington Avenue who liked to kill people and keep the Dominoes' books on one floppy disc. He'd turned the Dominoes into a multimillion-dollar gang with Swiss bank accounts, while the Jokers struggled to hold onto their cash.

"Jefe, you'll have to give me the guy with the blue mustache."

"What's his sin?"

"He raped an idiota . . . one of ours."

Martin Lima bounced the crack babies on his lap, and Bernardo had to interpret this gesture: the prince was angry at Panther, angry at Bernardo, angry at himself.

"If it's true, Dublin, I'll take care of it. I'm like King Solomon. I have my own tribunal. What's the idiota's name?"

"Jefe, it's Joker territory, and it has to be a Joker solution. That was part of our pact."

He brushed against one of the crack babies and pulled out the Glock from inside the strap on her thigh. Lima's driver lunged against Bernardo with his Nighthawk, but he was a little too late. Bernardo socked him on the side of the head, and the driver started to groan. The second crack baby reached for her Glock, and Bernardo slapped her hand away.

The prince was seething. "I made you rich . . . you cannot steal weapons from me in my own Cadillac."

"Jefe, what are you saying? I'm one of your loyal subjects. This gun has been blessed by a prince. I will blow out Panther's brains, and you will be the real executioner."

"Dublin, the Jokers will starve without me. Your banking practices stink."

"We're peasants. We never learned to handle money like a prince . . . your Dixie Cups weren't supposed to sell in the schoolyards, and rape retarded girls."

"Panther isn't a Dixie Cup. He's my captain."

"That's even worse, because his lack of respect came from you. Jefe, if you continue to break the hearts of our little mothers, I will find you and piss on your head in front of all the Dominoes. You'll run to Santo Domingo to hide from the shame."

Bernardo got out of the car, blew kisses into the glass, and watched Martin Lima drive away. Abdul crept up behind him.

"Take me to that fuck with the blue mustache."

They walked down the hill to Cromwell Avenue, where the Dominoes had established their own candy store on Joker land. Bernardo parked Abdul behind a lamppost and stepped into the candy store with the Glock wrapped in a handkerchief inside his pocket, while soldiers eyed him from the counter, Nighthawks in their hands. They all recognized Bernardo Dublin, the Bronx detective who'd made a treaty with their five princes. They couldn't even question him. Bernardo was walking too fast. And why should they get rough? He was the nearest thing to royalty the Jokers had. Bernardo didn't stop until he discovered the man in the blue mustache pondering a primitive slot machine. Martin Lima had swiped it from a smugglers' warehouse in lower Manhattan and had given the machine and a bucket of money from all over the world to Panther's candy store. But Panther, who was hairless except for his mustache, and had a slight hump, couldn't play "La Bandida." He tried to hypnotize the machine, put a spell on it with his milky eye, when Bernardo crept into Panther's feeble field of vision.

"Dublin, how's my man?"

Bernardo reached into the bucket, pulled out a coin, fed it into the machine, which lit up like a silver moon. He pulled on the lever, the wheels churned, and three painted oranges lined up in the window. La Bandida piped a little tune, and coins began to drop from its bowels into a metal tray.

"You're a bruja," Panther said. "Only a witch could open up La Bandida and make her part with her money."

"Yeah," Bernardo said. "I'm a bruja." He'd played a similar bandit at the casino in Deauville. But none of the Dominoes had ever been to Deauville, and they couldn't figure out that La Bandida would only feed on French coins.

Panther turned his back, yawned, and Bernardo realized that the prince had never even bothered to warn him, hadn't called the candy store. Bernardo swung him around delicately with one hand.

"Panther, you shouldn't have touched la idiota. She belongs to us."

And he glocked Panther, shot him in his milky eye. Panther's head exploded. He crashed into La Bandida, and more coins spilled into the tray. His soldiers seemed perplexed. They looked at Panther, looked at Bernardo Dublin, listened to the music of La Bandida, watched that continuing shower of coins . . . as if Panther, dead or alive, had magicked the machine. They hadn't quite recovered from their trance when Abdul leapt into the candy store with his glass gun. They dropped their own glass guns and pleaded with Bernardo.

"Jefe, don't kill us, please."

Bernardo smashed each of their Nighthawks against the counter, then he shoved the soldiers into the store's tiny toilet, and warned them not to leave for half an hour. He wiped the Glock, left it on top of La Bandida, walked behind the counter, and made a chocolate ice cream soda for Abdul and himself. His hands were trembling. He drank the soda, ate some pretzel sticks, and marched to the motel with Abdul. His hands were still trembling. Bernardo wasn't scared of his own skin. He'd gone into the candy store on Cromwell Avenue like any fucking warrior prepared to die. He stood under the shower. He was still shaking. He put on his pants and leather coat, got a little Polish vodka out of the fridge, and the trembling stopped. He turned around. She was standing near the mirror, wearing a velvet cloak, like a million dollars in a whores' motel.

"Fantômas," she said.

"Shut up."

"My Bronx baby is growing cross."

"It isn't safe here . . . did Abdul let you in?"

"Why shouldn't he let me in? I'm one more piece of ass."

"Don't say that."

"Then you shouldn't live here, Bernardo. Like a vagabond. Come downtown and stay with me."

"Yeah. Marianna would love that. The killer cop who jumps into her mama's pants."

"Marianna's nuts about you. She wishes she could live inside my pants."

"Don't say that. She's not a puta."

"We're all alike. Either angels or putas, aren't we, my Latin lover?"

"I'm half Irish," Bernardo had to insist.

"Then behave like an Irishman . . . put on your mask."

"No."

She started to undress, and Bernardo realized what all that trembling had been about. He didn't want to go to hell without Clarice. The thought of not making love to her again in *this* world terrified him. He didn't give a damn what he'd have to endure down below. Hot coals? Icicles on his ass? Rat's piss in his vodka cup? As long as he had Clarice here, now.

She swirled his vodka in her mouth. "Put on your mask."

"Then I might have to hurt you."

"I'll take my chances, darling. Put on your mask."

He fished out the hangman's hood from under his bed. He cursed the Big Guy who'd filled his brain with Fantômas. Sidel was always into masquerades. "There was a guy named Gurn," Isaac once said. "A lowlife, an artillery sergeant in the Boer War, with black powder on his face. That was Fantômas' first mask. He served under a nobleman, Lord Bentham, and fell in love with the nobleman's young wife. A beautiful creature, dark or blond, who cares? She could sink a whole continent with her looks. The lord finds his lady with that lowlife, points a pistol at Lady Bentham's heart. Gurn had no choice. He springs on Lord Bentham, strangles him, and grows into that curious king of crime, the aristocrat without a family tree, the man who turned his own history into fire and smoke . . ."

Bernardo had found the mask in the basement of a theatrical supply shop. There wasn't a single lowlife cop in Isaac's classes at the Academy who didn't long for the same magic transformation, coupled with murder. The anonymous artillery sergeant couldn't reinvent himself without taking the lady and strangling the lord.

Bernardo was naked all of a sudden, shivering at the beauty of *his* Lady Bentham. How many of her lords would he have to kill?

11

There was a spooky feeling on Featherbed Lane. Alyosha couldn't find one Dixie Cup. The streets were crystal clean, without a bubble pipe in anyone's mouth burning little white rocks. The Dominoes didn't cruise by in their Cadillacs. The traffic on the Cross Bronx seemed to mark its own quiet music, like drumbeats in the rain, only it wasn't raining, and Alyosha had to wonder if some poor prick had confused ratland with paradise. And then he realized what the quiet was all about. He saw ten Dominoes, not Dixie Cups, but warlords with their regular colors, gray neckerchiefs and gold bracelets, grouped like Apaches on top of the hill, not those false Apaches from the Bronx brigade but red-blood Indians who could really make you suffer.

Alyosha had nowhere to run, because ten other Dominoes had taken the street below him. And it wasn't any war game. These Apaches had come for Alyosha. They must have wanted some kind of revenge on the Joker's mural man. He didn't cry for Paulito. Paulito was stuck in a hole. But Alyosha couldn't imagine who would draw his own memorial. There wasn't enough talent in the Bronx to render his dark blue eyes. *Rest In Peace, Homey* . . .

The two bands arrived like a pair of pinchers, ready to squeeze Alyosha. Then a white Cadillac appeared out of its own crazy mirage, with the Domino flag hanging from the aerial: five black dots on a gray field. The door opened. Alyosha got inside with a couple of baby brujas who were already getting famous in El Bronx as gun molls; they would fire on cats and garbage cans while the white Cadillac cruised. But they didn't seem too interested in the sights of Featherbed Lane. They grabbed Alyosha, kissed him, touched his dick.

"Miranda, this one is cute. Are you sure he was a little puta at the boys' prison?"

"Sure I'm sure. He sucked every guard in the house."

The baby brujas giggled. And Alyosha was mortally wounded: he'd never gone near a guard . . . except when the older boys made him put on high heels and a dress.

"I dunno," said the second gun moll. "He don' look like no fairy to me."

And Alyosha rolled among them, helpless in their battlewagon. They bounced across the little Washington Bridge into Domino country, and Alyosha had that awful fear that he was back at Spofford again, having to parade in front of the older boys. But Spofford was at the other end of the world, in Hunts Point, near

Casanova Street, and Alyosha was heading toward Fort Washington Avenue, where the Dominoes had bought an abandoned supermarket and made it into their national headquarters.

The Cadillac drove into a tunnel that led right inside the supermercado, which was one enormous room with a bowling alley, a luncheonette, a little red-light district where the gun molls could lie down with favored warlords, a dance floor, a drug factory, a bank with its own vault, a dormitory where the Dixie Cups slept, and five silver thrones for the gang's five princes, but four of the princes must have been having their "periods," because only one throne was occupied. Martin Lima sat on the middle throne, with his warlords and business associates and baby brujas.

"Ah, maestro," he said to Alyosha, "glad you could make it."

Alyosha didn't know how to address a prince. He bowed, measured his words, and muttered, "How's His Highness?"

"High, man. Very high."

He handed Alyosha pieces of colored chalk and photographs of some mother in a blue mustache. "I mean, the Jokers can't monopolize you, kid. Talent is talent. It has to be shared . . . I want you to do a portrait of Panther on my wall. I have the right to ask. He was butchered by your brother's gang."

"But I need my paint bombs and a ladder."

"Nobody sprays paint in my supermercado. The cans could start a fire."

"Highness, I never painted indoors. I need natural light."

"We're drug merchants. We never leave this building except for a crisis. You'll have to live with our light . . . now begin!"

Alyosha had the whole rear wall. He grabbed a very fat stick of yellow chalk and sketched Panther's outline in five minutes flat. Then he reached across the wall and drew the brittle mountains of Washington Heights in the light of the moon. He applied the different colors, standing on his toes, chalked in Panther's blue mustache, the white of his milky eye, the gray of his handkerchief, the rough black teeth of rooflines under a renegade moon. He'd mastered the properties of chalk, teaching himself on the spot how to make a color bleed, so the blue of Panther's mustache could blend right into the atmosphere.

"Perfect," Martin Lima said. "Maestro, I'm touched that you could immortalize Panther like that . . . preserve his motherfucking essence, but you're still a Joker, and I can't forget that fact . . . Felipe, he's all yours."

Alyosha couldn't understand what Mouse's cousin was doing at the supermercado. Felipe had come out of Spofford, come out of the Bronx, to work for the Dominicans. He was fifteen years old. He smiled at Alyosha, approached him with a tube of lipstick.

"Jefe, I think I'll decorate the puta's mouth . . . then he can kiss all the boys and girls."

"What about the cucarachas?" one of the warlords shouted.

"Yes, the cucarachas too."

And Alyosha's premonition had been right. The supermercado was another Spofford. But he wasn't going to kiss or be kissed. He lunged at Felipe, stabbed him in the eye with the stick of blue chalk.

"Mama," Felipe said, "I'm blind."

The warlords and the baby brujas fell on top of Alyosha, began to kick him, scratch him, bite his face, until a figure in a mustard-colored shirt pulled Alyosha out from under all those bodies. It was Richardson of the Bronx brigade. He wore a cowboy hat in the supermercado.

Martin Lima shouted at him. "Brock, you're interfering with a Domino operation."

"Yeah, but he's my snitch, and I can't afford to lose him."

"The maestro works for you?"

"Everybody works for me, prince. You ought to know that."

"I don't care," Martin Lima said. "You'll have to ransom him."

"I'll ransom him with that," Richardson said, dangling his handcuffs.

"You threaten me, man, in my own living room?"

"Believe what you want, prince, but I can have my whole brigade here in half an hour."

"No," the prince said. "Never. They're strictly Bronx."

"All they have to do is close their eyes and cross a river."

"Let them cross. You're on my payroll. I can prove it with my own printout."

"Wrong," Richardson said. "You're one of my registered rats."

"Rat? I'll fix you."

"Relax," Richardson said. "You're part of my manhunt, prince. We're all trying to rid the Bronx of nefarious gangs like the Latin Jokers."

"Then how come the kid's alive? His brother runs the Jokers."

"Wrong again. I run the Jokers. And Alyosha's my little helpmate."

"That still doesn't make you innocent . . . Bernardo killed my captain."

"Panther? You're better off without him. And Bernardo had instructions from me."

"Are you crazy, man, to tell me this?"

"Panther was stealing from you, prince. Look what I found . . . after I searched the candy store."

He tossed a small grocery bag packed with hundred-dollar bills into Martin Lima's lap.

"Dummy," Richardson said, "the man had his own fucking bank inside the slot machine . . . he was a thief."

"He could have been holding that bag as part of a bigger payment."

"Correct. But the payment wasn't for you, homey. It was for Mr. Brock Richardson of the Bronx brigade."

"Talk my language, man, or get out."

"He was ambitious. He wanted your throne. He was getting up a bundle to pay Bernardo . . ."

"Pay him for what?"

"To sock one into you."

"Liar," Martin Lima said.

Richardson took out his pocket tape recorder, switched it on, and half the supermercado heard Panther's voice.

". . . I hate that fuck with the pockmarks. I get peanuts to do his dirty work. You wanna guess why all the other princes are on vacation?"

"Turn it off," the prince said.

Richardson dropped the recorder into his coat, tugged on Alyosha's sleeve, and left with him, while Martin Lima ranted into Richardson's back.

"Brock, nobody gave you or Dublin a license to hit my people . . ."

Richardson threw Alyosha into his mustard-colored Ford and started to laugh.

"Richardson, you're a genius. How'd you get that tape?"

Richardson rolled his eyes. "I wired the candy store, that's how."

"And Panther really paid . . ."

"He didn't pay shit. I spliced a few sentences together. And I created a little monologue of Panther raving against the prince."

"What about the bag of money?"

"The money's mine. I had to take the loss, or I couldn't have shocked the prince into believing all the bull I told him."

"It came out of your pocket?"

"Sixty grand. But I'll get it back."

"Richardson, I take back whatever bad things I said

about you. The hell with Merlin. I'm going to your school from now on."

The gangbuster slapped Alyosha on the head. "You'll do more than that, homey. You're gonna watch Bernardo, play up to him, kiss his ass."

"Bernardo's with your own brigade."

"He's a loose wire," Richardson said. "Has his own electric power . . . homey, who saved your life?"

"You did, Brock."

"And what do you owe me?"

"Everything."

"And what do you have to tell me?"

"Nothing, Brock."

He didn't tell Richardson about his meal with Marilyn the Wild, and the talk he'd overheard between Isaac and Barbarossa. He should have. Bernardo was a son of a bitch, an executioner. He'd sentenced David Six Fingers to death, had destroyed David's hobby shop. But Alyosha couldn't seem to talk about Fantômas, and some mask that made no sense . . .

Richardson didn't deliver him to Featherbed Lane. They didn't even return to the Bronx. They drove into the heart of Manhattan, and Richardson let him off in front of Marianna's building.

"You wait for Bernardo upstairs. He'll be coming back with his bitch. You do a little song and dance and when it's time to go, you can ride uptown with Bernardo. He'll open up to you, and then you can start pumping him."

"Pumping him about what?"

"The stars, the moon, and Clarice's tits . . . he talks, you listen. That's the business of a rat."

He handed Alyosha an enormous box of chocolates.

"Richardson, what's that?"

"I dunno. I found it near Panther . . . at the candy store. Give it to your sweetheart. That's why you're here, aren't you? The candy box is your cover, kid. You're courting Marianna Storm."

Alyosha went into the building. The doorman announced him, and he rode upstairs with a box of chocolates that was bigger than a barbell. Marianna met him at the door with a puzzled look.

"Alyosha, I didn't . . ."

"This is for you," he said, and she had to carry the chocolates. He followed her into the apartment and now he understood her embarrassment. Marianna had a guest, Tippy Goldstone, a fifteen-year-old footballer from Horace Mann. He had blond hair and wore the colors of his school. He stared at the chocolates and tried not to smirk.

"Tip," she said, "Alyosha's a great, great artist. He does unbelievable drawings . . . in the Bronx."

"I'd love to see them," Tip Goldstone said. "But tell me, 'Alyosha' isn't Bronx material. Is it your tag, your gang name?"

"No. I'm named after a moron in a Russian novel."

"I thought so," said Tip Goldstone. "*The Idiot*, isn't it?"

"No. *The Brothers Karamazov*."

"I'm fascinated . . ."

Marianna glowered at him. "Tippy, stop."

"I mean it. Mr. Alyosha, who gave you that name?"

"The Bronx brigade. I'm on their books as a registered rat."

Tip Goldstone grew alert. "Really?"

"I helped them put my brother in jail. They got to Rooster Ramirez and David Six Fingers on account of me . . . Mr. Goldstone, I kill whatever I touch."

Alyosha ran out of the apartment. Marianna followed him into the hall, with the chocolates against her chest. But she couldn't find Alyosha. He hadn't waited for the elevator. He took the stairs.

She returned to the apartment with Alyosha's chocolates.

"Quite a little character," said Tip. "If that's what Merlin is about, I'd like to join. But do you believe his tale?"

"Yes," Marianna said. "Every word." And she started to scream at Tip, who suddenly saw how much in love he was with Marianna. He took the chocolates out of her arms, tried to kiss her. Marianna socked him in the face. He stumbled for a moment, said "Marianna . . ."

She socked him again.

He started to sulk. He patted his Horace Mann jacket, turned on his heels like a cadet in a parade drill, and left.

Marianna sat down on the floor with her box of chocolates. Alyosha had to show up when Tippy was here. She didn't even like Tippy Goldstone. She was experimenting with a new kind of cookie, peanut brittle, with raisins, and she'd invited him on a whim.

Clarice arrived with Fantômas, discovered Marianna

on the floor. "Darling," she said, "are you doing aikido, or what?"

"I'm contemplating a box of chocolates. Can't you tell?"

She gave Fantômas a peanut brittle cookie and ran into her room.

12

He'd been trained by the Big Guy, and Bernardo could total a man in half a second, finesse a criminal into giving up his gun, and know when some fucker was following him. But this fucker was as shrewd as Bernardo himself, shrewder even, because his shadow didn't leave a trace. Bernardo had to sniff him in the wind, like a hunting dog. But the shadow had his own sixth sense. The fucker fell back, aware now that Bernardo was aware of him. It couldn't have been an ordinary cop, or an Apache from the basement at Boro Hall. Bernardo would have spotted one or the other. It had to be a cop from Bernardo's own class at the Academy, someone who'd also been trained by Sidel. Another fucking Fantômas.

Bernardo zigzagged across Manhattan, from Sutton Place South to Peter Cooper Village, then north and south again to the Lillian Wald projects, where he'd busted up a gang of Puerto Rican separatists while he was still at the Academy. Isaac had plucked him out of class and put him into the street. He'd lived under-cover for three months. The separatists were going to bomb the Statue of Liberty. Bernardo delivered them and all their sticks of dynamite. There was one more cop on the same assignment. A madman who had no fear of the separatists, who would have slept with dy-namite day and night, who'd come out of Vietnam with a slightly crippled hand . . .

Bernardo stopped at a bar on East Thirteenth, where the separatists had congregated once upon a time, drinking Scottish ale that they called TNT. Half a glass could fix you for the afternoon, make your eyeballs wander in your head, and give you enough vitamins and minerals so that you could skip two meals. The bar hadn't changed. Bernardo sat in the back with his TNT. He didn't even have to watch the window.

Vietnam Joe wandered in, ordered the same brown ale, and sat down with Bernardo. They clinked glasses without a smile.

"Hair of the dog," they said. Neither of them knew what it meant, but that's what all the separatists sang when they sipped TNT.

"When did you make me?" Barbarossa asked.

"I felt you, brother, I felt you for a long time."

"It's not official. I wouldn't wire you down for those crapheads at IAD."

"I know. You're with the glamour boys. I caught your picture in the *Post* . . . guarding Madonna. But I don't need a chaperone."

"Bernardo, the Big Guy depends on you. You're the

only thoroughbred he has. He can't run Merlin without you. And you pull a stunt that's like a textbook case from the Academy. You visit Storm's wife wearing a mask . . ."

"I'm kinky, and so is Clarice."

"Who paid you to put on that mask?"

"I told you, Joey. It's a sexual twist."

"Who wants her dead?"

"It's a mystery."

"How did we survive the separatists? We read each other's eyes in the dark. We never bullshitted each other . . . Bernardo, I can't read your eyes and I have so much light, I could be sitting in a sun-shower."

"It's my own caper, Joey. Tell that to the Big Guy."

"Tell him yourself. All you fucking Apaches ought to be in jail. Just tell the Big Guy what's behind your little romance."

"I can't."

"Bernardo, you're my only case right now. I'll dog you until one of us is dead."

"I know . . . would you care for another cup of TNT?"

They shared three more bottles, reminisced. Barbarossa had been Bernardo's hero, the street cop who'd sold drugs in Vietnam and would jump off a roof to catch a falling child.

"Joey, I've been remiss. I never gave you a wedding present."

"How could you? You're busy with the Bronx."

"It's a funny thing. I hate Manhattan. I get the hives soon as I hit Central Park. It was never that way.

Didn't we cruise the Village, Joey? Didn't we eat Peking duck with the biggest Chinese gamblers?"

"You've been an Apache too long."

"I always wanted to get out of the Bronx. I had the best ticket. Sidel. He sent me to Italy and England and France. The Grand Tour, he said. I was in Monaco and Deauville. I saw the leaning tower of Pisa. It's not a joke. That sucker really does lean. I visited castles. I gobbled snails. I saw the room where Leonardo da Vinci invented the airplane."

"He did not. It was the Wright brothers, Orville and Wilbur. I read it in a book. They climbed up into the air in the Kitty Hawk."

"Fuck Orville and Wilbur. Joey, I looked at da Vinci's drawings. I traced the outline of his flying ship with my own finger . . . lemme finish. After the tour, I couldn't bear Manhattan. That leaning tower belonged in the Bronx."

"I gotta blow. Search your stinking heart, huh? And be careful, kid. I'm not the only one who's following you. I noticed a couple of Apaches on your tail."

"Impossible," Bernardo said. "I would have made them in a minute."

"Not when they work in teams of nine and ten, each Apache with his own perimeter."

"Fuck their perimeters. Nobody else is on my tail. Only you."

"Bernardo," Barbarossa said, getting up from the table. "Listen and live. Go to Isaac before it's too late."

Bernardo sat alone, nursed the dregs of his TNT. He grew homicidal, thinking of Richardson and his old

Apache trick, ten cops with field radios while Bernardo walked in and out of their perimeters.

He rode uptown to Boro Hall, passing the deserted shell of Yankee Stadium. He'd been a little young to see Mantle and Maris in a Yankee uniform, though the Big Guy had taken him to the owners' box last year to meet the Mick, a jovial, aging bad boy with lines on his neck. The Big Guy was like a baby. He asked Mantle for his autograph, and he treasured that slip of paper, walked around with it, staring at Mantle's autograph, ignoring the governor of New York and two borough presidents.

Bernardo went up to Richardson's rooms. Richardson was smoking pot with his Apaches. Bernardo had to be polite. He sucked once on Richardson's roach. Then Richardson dismissed the other Apaches.

"Homey, I got you out of hot water. Martin Lima was getting ready to skin you alive."

"Watch me tremble," Bernardo said.

"You'll tremble, all right. I had to clean up your dirty deeds. The prince is paying good money. You didn't have to do bloody carnage in a candy store."

"And Panther didn't have to rape a retarded girl."

"You have to fold that into the profits. Every deal has a downside."

"She's in a coma, Brock."

"Then you ask my permission . . . and I would have given it. I told Lima that the decision to hit came from me."

"That's kind of you. But you'd better pull your boys, or I'll cripple them."

"What boys?" Richardson said, handling the roach with his special tweezers.

"I used to be part of that perimeter trick, remember? How many warlords did we destroy with our eight-piece band?"

"Eight? I had to put twenty Apaches on your ass, have them watch you around the clock. That's a compliment, homey."

"I'd call it the ground plans for a kill."

"Are you wearing a wire? Or are you just a psychopath? I'd caution you to shut your fucking mouth."

"Search me, Brock, pat me down."

"I don't have to search you. But you shouldn't have disappointed us. You were supposed to frighten that woman to death, throw her off the balcony if you had to, and you end up fucking her at every historical site in the Bronx. You're into me for ninety thousand."

"You'll get your money back."

"It's not about money. You had a deed to do. We can't risk a second attack. She'll get wise and go to the police. Or worse. She'll blab to the Big Guy."

"But she has nothing to blab about."

"Yeah, Bernardo. That's our problem. But you could do us a favor and keep away from the bitch. How can we plan anything if you're her bodyguard?"

"Don't hurt her, Brock."

"What?"

"I mean it. I don't want her touched."

"Are you getting Alzheimer's, kid? That woman is our ticket."

"Then you'll have to change your ticket."

"I could suspend your ass. I could give you eternal desk duty, without a gun."

"Come on, Brock. We're the good guys. We don't make war on each other. We only nuke the gangs, one by one . . . and live off their labor."

He wandered out of Richardson's offices. Apaches kept looking at him . . . he was already a pariah. He walked uptown to the motel. Abdul wasn't at the gate. Abner Gumm had found another kid. Bernardo couldn't recognize him, though the kid wore the blue handkerchief hat of the Jokers. A virgin, he muttered, a fresh recruit.

He met Abner in the common room of their bungalow. The Bronx historian had a twitch at the edge of his mouth.

"What's wrong, Shooter? Expecting company?"

"The streets are too quiet," Abner said.

"Then you ought to have a picnic photographing all the bricks and stones."

"In this haze? Even the rats would seem invisible."

Abner went into his own bedroom, shut the door. Bernardo watched an old movie on Abner's giant screen. With Gable. About an earthquake in San Francisco. And a woman who sings in Gable's saloon. She reminded him of Clarice. Jeanette MacDonald, who still had fan clubs all over the world . . .

Bernardo went into his own room. Took off his clothes, got into the shower. But he didn't like the movement at the corner of the Shooter's mouth. He didn't like not seeing Abdul at the gate, and he brought his Glock into the shower with him, propped it against the soap dish, where it wouldn't be wet. He sang a little louder than he should have. "San Francisco . . ."

He caught the shadow of a man through the shower curtain. He didn't stop singing. He grabbed his Glock and barreled through the curtain. Barbarossa was sitting in Bernardo's leather chair.

"Get dressed. You're gonna have some visitors."

Bernardo only had time to get into his underpants when three guys in hangman's hoods tiptoed into the room with Nighthawks. Bernardo almost laughed. A chorus of Fantômases. He didn't even consider glocking them. Barbarossa seized their glass guns while Bernardo tweaked their noses under the masks.

"Kid," Barbarossa said, "aren't you gonna look?"

"Why? It will make me sick."

It was Barbarossa who plucked off the masks. He saw three brats with burnt lips and ragged eyes. Dixie Cups? Kamikazes who'd taken long blows on their pipes? Who else would run into Bernardo Dublin's bedroom?

"Ah, Joey, tell them to scram. They're Dixie Cups, very, very low on the ladder."

He shoved the three Fantômases out of the room with their Nighthawks . . . and the Shooter came in clutching a baseball bat. Bernardo smiled at the signature: Roger Maris. A Yankee fan, through and through.

The twitch was gone from the Shooter's face. "Bernardo, I was sleeping . . ."

"It's all right, Ab. Lemme introduce you to Barbarossa, Sidel's son-in-law."

"Ah, I met Sidel," the Shooter said. "He invited me to the mansion."

"Dad's like that. He loves to mingle."

"It wasn't a social call. He asked me lots of questions. I'm the Bronx's official historian."

"Of course. Abner Gumm. I admire your photographs. I saw them on Fifth Avenue. At the museum."

"All right," Bernardo said. "Ab, go back to your bedroom . . . and thanks for bringing the Roger Maris."

The Shooter left, and Bernardo began to pace. "Joey, I don't wanna hear one word . . . I'm not talking to Isaac. I'm not talking to you. Now I'd like to finish my shower, okay?"

He crept back inside the curtain . . . without his Glock. He'd lied to Barbarossa. He recognized the three little shits. They belonged to Richardson's crop of rats. His boss had sent him a kiss and a kite. *Careful, Bernardo. The Apaches are coming.*

Part Four

13

Isaac arrived in a police launch at the fireboat station and raced across Carl Schurz Park to meet with the Merliners. He'd been attending a conference at the Children's Psychiatric Center on Wards Island. He'd argued with every doctor in the house. He wanted to board violent children upstairs at Gracie Mansion. "I'll cure them."

"Your Honor, the City wouldn't allow it."

"I'll pay for their keep out of my own pocket."

"It's still illegal," said the chief psychiatrist. "There's no supervision, nothing."

And he crossed Hell Gate on the police launch in time for Merlin. But Alyosha wasn't there and Isaac began to brood. He'd become a cracked patriarch, believing that all the kids in the City belonged to him.

Marianna seemed as disappointed as Isaac. She'd baked peanut brittle cookies for the Merliners, but she wouldn't sample them without Alyosha. Even Isaac seemed reluctant: he couldn't feast without the kid. But one of the guests was having a jolly time. Porter Endicott, the president of his family's own private bank. He kept gobbling Marianna's cookies. He was thirty-six years old, the chairman of Billy the Kid's treasure chest and the only banker around that Isaac could bear. He'd been using his family's fortune to build playgrounds in the Bronx. But he wouldn't invest in local enterprises or local housing.

Isaac had invited him to talk with the Merliners. He looked like a bum next to the young banker.

"Why playgrounds, Porter, when you won't help struggling businessmen?"

"It's simple. The money for the playgrounds comes out of my own pocket. I don't expect a return in capital. I'm investing in kids who will use the basketballs I donate."

"But you're not concerned about where they live, or whether their moms and dads can find a job."

"I am concerned," Porter said, "but I can't blind myself, I can't piss away capital. The Bronx is a bad risk at best."

"Couldn't you encourage small businessmen?"

"I do. But not with the bank's money."

"For Christ's sake, Porter, give the fucking borough a chance to survive."

Porter bit into another cookie. "You ought to watch your language, Mr. Mayor. We're among children."

"Ah," Isaac said, "they know me by now . . . I get excited. I curse. It means nothing."

"But it means something to me. Respect that."

"Sorry," Isaac said. "Merliners, I apologize."

"Cure the problem, Mr. Mayor. You can't even count on the Yankees anymore."

"Should I kidnap J. Michael Storm?"

"No. Just have his daughter deny him her cookies for life."

"I don't bake cookies for Dad," Marianna said. "I never did. But Uncle Isaac is right. Your bank ought to have deeper pockets."

"I wish it could. But I'd have to see other signs of caring, other signs of life . . . it's a question of supply and demand, and the Bronx has too little of each."

"There's lots of supply where I come from, and even more demand," said Bernardo Dublin, who'd arrived from the Castle Motel in a red vest, a fury in his pale green eyes. "We're plenty rich, and we have our own bankers."

"Rich in what?" Porter asked, ready to bait a half-breed cop.

"Rocks," Bernardo said.

"Ah, we're studying geology now. Bronx sandstone and schist."

"No. I'm talking crack, the real economy of El Bronx. Drugs, Mr. Endicott, which are sold in the playgrounds you build."

"Bernardo," Isaac said, "that isn't fair. Cut it out."

"Let him finish," the banker said.

"Money flows right off the street . . . it circulates from fist to fist. It requires a glass pipe and a little blow-torch."

"Ah, the underground growth of the Bronx."

"It isn't so underground, Mr. Endicott."

"And I should finance factories in the middle of gang wars."

"The gangs have their own factories," Bernardo said. "They don't need any of yours."

"And what are you doing about it, Detective Dublin?"

"It's business, just like your bank. When you have a buyer, a seller will always appear."

"Didn't I tell you?" Porter said. "The cops are asleep . . . or corrupt."

"They're both," Bernardo said.

Isaac shuffled between them. "That's enough."

Bernardo smiled. "Not everyone's fortunate enough to have Isaac as a mentor. He took me off the street. But the cops are only chameleons. They reflect what the whole society wants them to reflect . . . nobody cares about El Bronx, so it cares about itself."

"And what do you propose I do?"

"Nothing," Bernardo said. "You couldn't change the street with all the playgrounds in the world."

"Bernardo," Isaac said.

"Boss, should I dance, should I sing? Should I entertain the Merliners with lovely little lies?"

"I'm not your boss," Isaac said. "I'm a mayor with a mansion, that's all. And Porter is our guest."

"Then let him act like one."

The Merliners clustered around Porter Endicott, who'd come with gifts from his own bank, pen and pencil sets with the Endicott logo: a long silver line. But Marianna kept away from him. She wasn't in the mood for pens and pencils. She wanted Alyosha.

Isaac ground his teeth and whispered in Bernardo's ear. "Did you have to go and antagonize him, huh? He's our only friend on the Financial Control Board."

"He still sucks."

"And you're a sweetheart, huh? My big idealist. Do you have something to tell me, Bernardo? About Clarice?"

"I'm in love with the lady."

"And you didn't come into the picture wearing a mask?"

"If I did, boss, I copied from you . . . we're both Fantômas freaks."

"Go back uptown and find Alyosha. He should have been here."

"Maybe the kid doesn't like meetings."

"But he likes Marianna enough to tolerate them. He's crazy about her cookies. Alyosha's in trouble. I can feel it in my bones."

"Isaac, have I ever let you down? I'll find Alyosha."

And Bernardo skulked out of the mansion in his red vest.

The Merliners disbanded, and Isaac drove Marianna downtown with Porter Endicott. "I'm worried," she said. "Where's Alyosha?"

"I sent in my best scout. Bernardo."

"I'm worried," she said. She kissed Isaac on the cheek, shook Porter's hand, and ran into her apartment building on Sutton Place South. Isaac continued down to Pine Street and Porter's bank, which sat in a modest brownstone that had been put up during the Civil War, when Porter's great-granduncles gobbled up Manhattan real estate and British cotton mills.

They had an early dinner in the executive dining room, without another banker in sight. But a fat man in a blue blazer joined them in the middle of the meal. Tim Seligman of the Democratic National Committee, a former pilot in Vietnam who was the Party's kingmaker, financial wizard, and whip. He had a grilled steak with half a jar of mustard and a bottle of Canadian beer.

Isaac didn't talk politics. He ate in silence until dessert: a chocolate cake drenched in vanilla sauce.

"Tim, I won't back the Gov until you tell me what happened to Margaret Tolstoy. Did Billy the Kid ask the FBI to steal her from me?"

"Billy doesn't have the brains to ask."

"Then why the hell are you backing him for President?"

"Because he's a new face, and only a new face can win."

"Then who kidnapped Margaret?"

"I did," Seligman said.

Isaac shoved away the vanilla sauce. "Timmy, I could crack your windpipe with one hand. That's all I need."

"Isaac, she would have compromised our campaign."

"I don't give a fart about your campaign."

"Then you shouldn't have decided to go and live in a glass house. Sooner or later, Margaret Tolstoy would have been noticed. That woman has too many skeletons in her closet."

"And Billy's pure, I suppose. He had a black prostitute murdered."

"Isaac," Seligman said, "did you have to use the 'm' word? There could be microphones in the chandelier."

"Tim, I swear to God, he—"

"I don't want to hear about it," Seligman said, finishing his piece of cake.

"Where is she, Tim? Where's Margaret?"

"Out of the country. Safe . . . Isaac, you're in the ball game now, and it's a little too late to run out of the park. Besides, we wouldn't let you."

"Where is she?"

"In Prague. She attends dinner parties with the cultural attaché."

"Seligman, I'll cripple you, Billy, and that cultural attaché . . . I'll devour Prague until I find her. I'm getting on a plane."

"Great idea. We'll lend you a ticket. And Margaret Tolstoy won't survive your phantom visit to Prague."

"Let it rest," Porter said. "The woman's alive, and one day you'll get her back . . . we're giving the Bronx to you. My bank is prepared to move in. We'll buy up housing stock, rebuild the area around Yankee Stadium."

"And why are you so fucking generous all of a sudden?"

"Generous, Isaac? I always make a profit. And Billy can throw the first ball on Opening Day."

"There might not be an Opening Day."

"Leave that to us," Seligman said.

"And J. Michael Storm," Isaac said, getting up and rushing out of the room. He wanted to summon his chopper, return to the sky, sit above the rooftops of Featherbed Lane, catch Alyosha, but he had to attend a fund raiser in Queens and drink coffee with a band of firemen in Flatbush. The firemen were threatening to decapitate Republicans with their hooks, and Isaac couldn't abandon them to their own enthusiasm. He was a prancing white parade horse, a democratic horse.

14

The Mouse was haunting him from the grave, and it didn't matter how many murals Alyosha did. Mousy's cousin Felipe had snitched on him, had told every gang in the Bronx that Angel Carpenteros, aka Alyosha, was Richardson's registered rat. Scouting parties from the Malay Warriors, the San Juan Freaks, and the Jokers themselves had begun searching for Alyosha. He couldn't even go home. Two of the Jokers' baby hit men were patrolling Mt. Eden Avenue and Featherbed Lane. They'd already erased his signature from Rooster Ramirez' mural. Alyosha had become the boy without a country, banished from El Bronx.

Paulito would protect him, force the baby hitters and the scouting parties to go away. But what could Paulito do from his dungeon at Rikers? And then Alyosha realized that the baby hitters wouldn't be here without Paulito's approval. His brother had sent them to take revenge on the rat. Alyosha started to cry. He'd shamed Paul, made him look stupid in the eyes of his own gang. The supreme general of the Latin Jokers couldn't even count on the loyalty of his little hermano.

Where could Alyosha hide? In the elephant house at the Bronx Zoo? Elephants were as smart as people. They'd figure out that they had a spy among them, the little fink of Featherbed Lane. And then he saw Paulito in his blue handkerchief hat. His brother could fly through prison walls. Paulito was as much a magician as the Big Guy.

Paulito talked to the baby hitters, told them not to puff on their glass pipes in front of little kids. Alyosha was crouching behind a garbage barrel, pinned between the hitters and a couple of scouting parties. *Paulito*, he screamed inside his throat. But nothing came out, not the slightest peep.

Richardson made me do it. He got me out of Spofford. I couldn't spend my life sucking dicks.

Alyosha wouldn't have cared so much if Paulito glocked him, but he didn't want to get killed by baby hitmen, and what if Paulito gave them the order to shoot? That was a Bronx rule. The supreme general wasn't allowed to kill a rat with his own gun.

Paulito.

He'd never be able to live with Paulito again. He wanted to show off the espresso machine he'd bought with mural money while his brother was in the can. They couldn't even share a cup of coffee together. That's what happened when you married up with the Bronx brigade. You ended in the crapper every time.

Alyosha counted to ten, slipped away from the barrel, camouflaged himself against a broken wall, ducked into the cellar, came out behind his own building, on Hawkstone Street, where there wasn't a single posse, and he could buy twenty minutes before he zigzagged through the back yards, crept under the Cross Bronx, and hid out with the stray dogs near the Park Avenue railroad tracks . . .

Paulito sniffed burning coffee while he unlocked the door. It was almost as good as smack. In the old days, before there was an anti-gang brigade at the County Building, and the Jokers ruled El Bronx from Third Avenue to the Harlem River, Paulito could get high sucking in the aroma of Cuban coffee. But there weren't Dixie Cups on Joker soil, or hot bubble pipes that could scar your face. Paulito had never sold drugs. He'd let the shit pass through his territories, protect a couple of dealers, but it was wholesale; now there were Dixie Cups all over the place.

"Homey," someone called, "come on in. I was expecting the little brother, hoping for him. The kid has a mean coffee machine. I like to stop here for some brew."

Bernardo was standing in the kitchen with a contraption that Paulito hadn't seen before. "You haven't iced Angel, have you? It would break the Big Guy's heart, and I'd have to blow your head off."

"Angel?" Paulito said. "You mean Alyosha, the rat who helps destroy his own brothers and then draws their pictures on a wall."

"They would have been destroyed with or without him. The Jokers are a relic, all the gangs are."

"Thanks to you, Bernardo, one of our wise men. You sold us to the Dominoes and the Bronx brigade."

"Get modern," Bernardo said. "We couldn't exist on our own. All we had left was a label. Latin Jokers. Don't you watch the news? Everything is merger now and corporate raids. Paulito, the gang doesn't have a dime . . . how did you buy your way out of the hole?"

"I borrowed twenty thousand from the Dominoes, bribed a couple of screws. If I'm not back in twenty-four hours, they'll grab every Joker on the Island and feed them to the fist fuckers."

"And you think Martin Lima runs a charity ward? He lent you the twenty so you could find your own fucking grave on the street. Without you around, he can swallow the Jokers . . . I'm taking you back to Rikers."

"Not until I sentence Alyosha. He has to pay for his crimes."

"That's pathetic. Ask a twelve-year-old kid to face a firing squad. I'm taking you back to Rikers."

Bernardo handed him a cup of coffee. Paulito took a sip and said, "Fuck you."

"Can't you listen? You don't have a career as a general without the hole. Solitary is your last protection."

"Come on. Blow my brains out. Isn't that what Richardson is paying you to do?"

Bernardo felt a shiver at the back of his neck. If he hadn't been warring with the brigade, Richardson might have sent him to finish off Paulito between cups of coffee. Generals were becoming obsolete in the Bronx.

"Paulito, I beg you, stay off the street . . . and forget Alyosha. The kid worships you. They locked him in Spofford, made him wear a dress. He was half crazy when I found him. If you have to punish someone, punish me."

"Who did that to Angel?"

"I don't know. One of Mousy's cousins."

"And the Mouse didn't interfere? Then I'm glad he's dead."

"You won't hurt Alyosha?"

"He has to confess. The whole fucking thing. Bring him to me, Bernardo, before my own hitters get him."

"Can't you call off those little lunatics?"

"No," Paulito said. "It wouldn't be ethical. First I have to hear Angel's story."

"And you won't leave this crib?"

"I can't promise," Paulito said.

Bernardo finished his coffee and went into the street. He'd have to maneuver around the gangs, steer them in the wrong direction, and come up with Alyosha. He'd only gone a block when he could feel that faint imprint of the Apaches. Were they going to trample him in some quiet corner? Bernardo welcomed the chase. He'd rip through the Bronx, then double back to Boro Hall, avoid the elevators, sneak into Richardson's rooms, set his hair on fire, watch Richardson have a heart attack. But Bernardo couldn't afford to dream like Fantômas. His mind was playing tricks. Richardson would surround himself with Apaches, remain deep within his own perimeter, until Bernardo was out of the way.

He'd wavered too long. Fantômas never stops, Sidel had said at the Academy. "His real mask is his movement. He's always outside the expectation of your reach." And Bernardo hadn't reached fast enough. Five Apaches jumped out of the gloom, dragged him into one of their mustard-colored Fords, knocked him on the head, delivered him to a storefront on College Avenue, where they liked to interrogate prisoners of war, luckless gang leaders who wouldn't come over to their side.

"Look at Fantômas," the Apaches said. Their chief, Birdy Towne, had also graduated from Isaac's classes at the Academy. He was long, lean, and blond. It was Birdy who'd glocked Rooster Ramirez, who'd battled children for the Bronx brigade. And Bernardo could see his own face in the mirror of Birdy's eyes.

"Ah, you're wondering about Barbarossa. He'll be a little late. We gave him four flat tires under the El."

"Where's Brock?"

"Brock? He couldn't make it, love. But he sends his best."

And the Apaches began to sock him from five directions. They wouldn't even let him fall. Each of them cradled Bernardo in his arms, while the others punched and kicked . . . and then passed Bernardo on to the next Apache. He had to swallow his own blood or stop breathing. His mouth hurt, or he might have smiled. Brock had decided to skip Bernardo's little inauguration.

"When it's all over, Birdy, will you do me a favor and close my eyes," he said, between bites of blood. "I wouldn't want to waste a whole eternity looking at these walls."

"Don't be grim," Birdy said. "We aren't cop killers, are we, boys?"

"No, Birdy," the other four Apaches said.

"We're going to paralyze you, that's all. Take away your power of speech. Kick your brains in a little bit."

And he could barely remember the punches and kicks that followed, as if he'd become a kind of feather bed, a magical quilt that could absorb any blow. He must have dropped into a very light sleep, because he could hear the five Apaches laugh, call him Fantômas. Then a door slammed and they were gone and Bernardo couldn't move.

Somebody blinked above him. He could see Barbarossa through the blood in his eyes.

"Don't talk," Barbarossa said. "I failed you, kid. I fucked up. I wasn't clever. They rocked me around in their own cradle, sent me on a wild-goose chase, when I should have stuck close to you . . . don't talk. I'll take you to the hospital."

"Joey," Bernardo said.

"Jesus, kid. It's like your bones are made of glass. I'm scared to pick you up. I'll call an ambulance."

And Bernardo remembered the tale Isaac had told in class, how Fantômas had survived a terrible beating near London Bridge. Some crooked cops wanted to dispatch the king of crime, take on his infinite territories, become the new Fantômas. But the harder they kicked him, the quicker he rose; their very labor seemed to fuel Fantômas, and the crooked cops had to walk away. Fantômas found them, cut their throats.

"Joey, I aint no glass man."

"Don't talk," Barbarossa said. "Your teeth are falling out."

"Let them fall."

Brock Richardson had gone to another inauguration, and Bernardo had to get there. "Mt. Eden Avenue," he whispered in Barbarossa's ear. Barbarossa wrapped him in the blanket he usually saved for Isaac Sidel, and drove Bernardo to Mt. Eden Avenue. Bernardo wouldn't let another cop carry him up the stairs. He climbed, with both hands on the banister rail, arrived at Paulito's door, entered, and found Paulito. The Joker's general was sitting on the couch, with his hands in his lap, like he was going to church. But his eyes were swollen and there were deep red marks around his neck. The Bronx brigade had knocked him to the floor, strangled him, and then propped him on the couch, like a calling card.

"Joey," Bernardo said, "get him an ambulance, and then take me to Sidel."

"You're going to the hospital, kid, after I attend to this."

"Fuck the hospital. I'm Fantômas," Bernardo said and dropped right into the general's lap.

15

The hospital had very strange pictures on the wall: men with muttonchops and high, starched collars, and Bernardo wondered if this hospital was also a museum. There was a bird outside his window. Bernardo saw grass, a strip of water, a fireboat, and he understood whose museum he was in. All the muttonchops were mayors out of the City's past. Bernardo was in a back bedroom at Gracie Mansion, tucked away from ordinary traffic, the mayor's secret guest.

He had a hospital tray on his bed, with a glass of juice and some chocolate drink that was probably packed with protein. His mouth was too raw, he realized, to suck in solid food.

There was a long velvet pull near his bed, like in an older time, when one of the muttonchops might have slept here or at another mansion, and Bernardo tugged at it, gave it a terrific yank, because Birdy hadn't kept his promise and paralyzed him.

The Big Guy came running with Barbarossa.

"Boss, did you find Alyosha?"

"You're not allowed to talk. Your mouth is broken."

"Then Bernardo Broken Mouth is asking . . . where the fuck is Alyosha?"

"I've been in the sky all afternoon searching for the kid. I scoured the Bronx with Joe. There wasn't a sign of Alyosha."

"Boss, you want my opinion? You put too much faith in helicopters. You have to go on the ground."

"Shhh," the Big Guy said. "I had the cook prepare you a tub of lime Jell-O. It's soothing for the tonsils."

"I hate Jell-O. It's for octopuses . . . where's Paulito?"

"The coroner has him."

"And I suppose the perp is a fucking mystery out of Fantômas."

"It's no mystery to me," Barbarossa said. "It has all the earmarks of the Bronx brigade."

"Then why don't you arrest Richardson, close him down?"

"Because then we'd have to arrest you, and Dad won't listen. He thinks the Merliners would mourn you. It would leave a bad impression."

"And what do you think, Joey?"

"I would have flopped you and the whole brigade months ago."

The Big Guy sipped from Bernardo's juice. "I started that brigade when I was Commish. I handpicked every cop . . . knew half of them from the Academy."

"Like Birdy Towne and me."

"And what did both of you do?"

"We started killing kids."

The Big Guy spilled juice on his pants. "Joey, he's a Judas . . . I want him out of this room. Pack his bags and throw him to the dogs."

"Dad, he doesn't have any bags."

"Bernardo, I trusted you, I brought you into my own brood. You were supposed to work with the gangs, calm them down, not annihilate them."

"Boss, it comes to the same thing."

"In your miserable dictionary, not in mine . . ."

"We were everybody's darlings for a little while. Remember that documentary on ABC about the brigade, our sports program, our record arrests? What did they call us, Isaac? Pioneers and saints."

"You were making progress . . . wasn't he, Joey? I could feel the dent. The gangs were playing basketball with young cops, going to Yankee games together."

"And lighting up in the grandstands, doing dope."

"That was part of the recreation. Homicides were down sixteen percent. And then what happened?"

"Reporters stopped coming to the Bronx."

"It's not about popularity," the Big Guy said. "It's about kids and cops."

"But it was already too late. We set up phony drug deals, shot a couple of people. We were high morning and night. We'd invent a shitstorm and float out of it, bodies at our feet."

"And the gangs became your personal clay pigeons."

"Boss, it gets expensive to supply a whole brigade with grass. Richardson went into real estate, not to make a fortune, just to give us an edge. But prices in the Bronx kept going down and down, and we had to feed off the gangs . . ."

"Gimme your shield," the Big Guy said.

Barbarossa had to interrupt him. "Dad, you already have it. I put it in your drawer. You were holding it for Bernardo."

"I'll rip his face with it. I'll scar the fuck . . . who bankrolled your little empire?"

"Prince Martin Lima. Richardson would buy up abandoned buildings, rehab them, and Lima would shove in some of his own clients, but we still couldn't collect the rent . . ."

"Richardson's another John Jacob Astor, huh? The biggest landlord in the Bronx."

"He started a corporation, Sidereal Ventures."

"What the hell is that?"

"Sidereal, boss. It means blessed with stars, heavenly bodies. We all bought shares in Sidereal. I'm into Richardson for ninety or a hundred thou, and I'm not even sure how much he owes the prince. But the prince needed more territories for his product . . ."

"And you offered him the Bronx. You cleaned out the gangs so his Dixie Cups would have a free ride."

"I'm still poor as a mouse."

"Poorer," the Big Guy said. "Because I'll sink you, Bernardo, without a pension, without your Glock."

"Boss, can I keep the mask?"

"Joey, let's smother him, please. I'll put the pillow over his head. You hold his feet."

"Dad, he was your prize pupil."

"It doesn't mean a thing. Bernardo betrayed us . . ."

"Then ask him about Clarice."

The Big Guy patted his wet pants. "It's not my business if he wanted to throw Clarice off her balcony."

"Ask him, Dad."

"All right . . . Bernardo, who hired you to play Fantômas?"

"Richardson. He was acting as the prince's agent."

"I must be dense," the Big Guy said. "What does a Dominican druglord have to do with Clarice?"

"The prince is multinational. He has accounts everywhere. Switzerland. Florida. Texas. Brazil. And one of his hotshot attorneys is J. Michael Storm."

"Don't bullshit me," the Big Guy said. "J. Michael was a Maoist. He wouldn't go to bed with Martin Lima."

"It aint illegal. J. Michael moved the prince's money around, and the prince was doing him a little favor, helping him get rid of Clarice. Or maybe he thought it was a favor. I didn't discuss it with J. Richardson told me to get her out of Manhattan, and he didn't seem to care if she had to lie down in a wooden box."

"Why didn't he ask Birdy to do it? Birdy would have been a little more discreet. Clarice had never seen his face."

"But I knew the lay of the land. I tried to scare her . . . she laughed. I made love to her in the mask. That's when Marianna came in."

"And all the Merliners live happily ever after . . . except for Alyosha." The Big Guy nudged his son-in-law. "Joey, we have work to do. I'm dismantling the Bronx brigade. It was my dreamchild. I'm dismantling it."

"The two of us, Dad, against Richardson's Apaches."

"Didn't Fantômas take over the British police, turn it on its head, lead his own false attack against himself? We'll do the same to Richardson."

"And what about Bernardo?"

"Leave him here. He's my prisoner," the Big Guy said, and vanished from the bedroom with Joe Barbarossa, and Bernardo had to imagine Fantômas in muttonchops, like the mayors of New York, impersonating some police general, getting his own cops dizzy, exhausting them with chases across the roofs against a Fantômas who was right among them, at their very middle.

16

They couldn't find a single Apache. Richardson had forsaken his offices near the roof of the Bronx County Building. Isaac stared at mustard-colored walls and the lone secretary Richardson had left behind.

"He's incommunicado, Mr. Mayor. Out in the field. On a very big case. Any messages?"

"Yes. Tell Brock I love him, love him very much."

They stopped across the street, at the Concourse Plaza, where Maris and Mantle had lived with the rest of the New York Yankees, where Harry Truman had once taken a nap. It was now an old-age home, with chicken wire embedded in every window to discourage cat burglars and thieves. The mayor had promised to meet with certain pensioners who'd formed their own Isaac Sidel fan club. They knew Isaac's history better than he did, and they sat bundled down in sweaters and revisited his life.

"Isaac, tell the truth, your biggest satisfaction, after

Marilyn the Wild, wasn't winning elections or catching crooks, or even riding in your helicopter."

"My courses at the Academy, that's what I miss the most. I feel deprived without a classroom, condemned to some strange planet where no one has ever heard of blackboards and chalk."

"What's so special about teaching cops?"

"Ah, but they weren't cops in my classroom. They didn't even wear a gun. We didn't talk about crime scenes and medical examiners and morgues."

"Then what did you talk about?"

"Metaphysics," Isaac said. "All the laws that govern your ability to live inside your own skin."

"Laws," said a retired judge. "If we knew the laws, we wouldn't be at the Concourse Plaza. We'd be sailing on a yacht with other millionaires . . . and your cops wouldn't be cops. They'd throw off their uniforms and move to Wall Street."

"And bore themselves to death. They'd be back in my classroom after six months. Cops have a particular rush, a hot melody that invades their blood, and they can't find it anywhere else . . . ask Joe."

The pensioners looked at Barbarossa, recognized him as the cop who'd lived like an outlaw until he married Marilyn the Wild.

"Dad's right," Barbarossa said. "I'd get lonesome without the street."

A man in old clothes appeared with a box camera. He stooped around the pensioners, photographed them with Isaac and Barbarossa. It was Abner Gumm, the Bronx historian. Isaac wanted to smile and welcome

Gumm, but he couldn't. His natural nosiness got in the way, made him realize that Gumm was no accident. The Bronx historian had followed him here.

"Dad," Barbarossa whispered, "that's the Shooter. I met him in Bernardo's bungalow. Said he'd been to Gracie Mansion. I think he's full of shit. He comes running with a baseball bat after three Dixie Cups try to off Ber—"

"Joey, whose signature was on the bat?"

"What's the difference, Dad? My story isn't about baseball."

They had to stop whispering in front of the pensioners and Abner Gumm. Isaac fielded questions about the baseball war in the Bronx, but he couldn't fool his own fan club. His face had turned dark.

"Your Honor, don't deny us Yankee Stadium. It's the last excursion we have left. All we have to do is walk down the hill."

"I can't promise when the Yankees will play again."

"Don't promise. Just arrest all the players, force them to get into a uniform."

"But they haven't committed a crime."

"Yes they have. They took our pleasure away."

Isaac had tea and cookies with his fan club. But the cookies couldn't compare to Marianna's mocha chip and peanut brittle. He had to find Alyosha, or she'd never bake again.

Abner cornered him near a window. Isaac had to watch the world through chicken wire. But that imprisoned glass seemed to soothe him more than the picture of Hell Gate he had from his bedroom window.

"Hello, Shooter," Isaac said. "Did you have a chance to look at those murals I told you about? On Featherbed Lane."

"I've been busy doing portraits," Gumm said. "I'm studying senior citizens throughout the Bronx."

"That's kind of you," Isaac said. "Are you fixing our future, Ab? Are we gonna be seniors together at the Concourse Plaza? I can't wait."

Isaac hugged the members of his fan club and left with Barbarossa.

"He's spying on us for Richardson, isn't he, Dad? I could throw him off the roof."

"And leave the Bronx without an historian?"

They trudged down the hill into that heartland of housing projects and half-burnt buildings that had become a new kind of calvary for the Bronx. The poor were firebombed out of their homes, and that's how the Latin Jokers had been born, as baby arsonists for landlords who wanted to collect insurance money on buildings they no longer cared about. But the Jokers, under Bernardo Dublin, had imaginative minds. They weren't so eager to watch the Bronx burn. "We aint cannibals," Bernardo told the gang. "If we're gonna burn, let's burn other people's shit, not ours." And the Jokers put on their handkerchief hats and started hunting the landlords, threatened to firebomb them out of their own little mansions in the North Bronx unless the landlords paid the Jokers a monthly stipend. "College money," Bernardo called it. That's what he told Isaac when they first met. The Big Guy had come to speak at Bernardo's high school. And Bernardo, who was a terrible truant, attended classes that day. He was curious to hear a police chief. He'd made a tiny smoke bomb, a "toy" to blow Isaac out of the auditorium, but Isaac took all his confidence away. "Claim the Bronx," Isaac said. "It's your borough."

Isaac remembered the tall, muscular kid who came up to him after his speech. They had coffee together at a Bronx diner, and Isaac had a revelation: this kid ought to be a cop . . .

He crossed the railroad tracks with Barbarossa, entered Claremont Village, the most notorious housing project in the world, where warlords patrolled the roofs with assault rifles and enormous searchlights on wheels, without the usual hierarchy of a gang. They weren't vulnerable to any outside influence. Dixie Cups never came here. These warlords would have eaten up Richardson's Apaches and Prince Martin Lima. They had their own anarchic order that didn't relate to the rest of New York. They feuded among themselves, shot at each other from the roofs, carried crazy banners and flags. They didn't need murals to memorialize their dead, and they didn't need the City's services. They buried fallen warlords in the basement and never bothered about a death certificate. They seemed to have a fondness for Sidel, who hadn't disturbed them when he was Commish. It would have taken an army to unhouse the warlords, and even if Isaac could have found that army, half the women and children of Claremont Village would have been killed.

He stood in Claremont's common garden, which was cluttered with debris, and waited until one of the searchlights blinked at him, and then he rode up to the roofs with Barbarossa.

"Dad, it could get delicate. These birds don't know me."

"Ah, you're family. They wouldn't touch a hair on your head."

Isaac had already been up to the roofs, but it was Joe's first trip, and he kept looking at the warlords' little wonderland, a beehive of glass huts where they could sunbathe and sell drugs. The warlords had built a curious Copacabana above the dunes of the Bronx, a bone-dry beach whose surface was made of cement.

The oldest warlord on the roof was African Dave, who was twenty-nine, like Bernardo, and had been at Claremont Village most of his life. He'd survived because he had a modicum of manners: he wouldn't shine his searchlight in another warlord's face. He'd been wounded six or seven times, a white man who wore an Afro and lived around Latinos and blacks.

"Isaac, is that your son-in-law who still holds the record for selling more cocaine than any other cop, dead or alive?"

"That's him," Isaac said. "Barbarossa."

Dave shook Barbarossa's hand. He had battle scars under his eyes and mouth. He could have been a phantom who'd come walking out of a fire.

"I think I'll move all my shit," Dave said. "I'm sick of the landscape. Look what I have to wear?" He tugged at his fiberglass vest. "How long can I stay bulletproof?"

"Where are you going, Dave?"

"To Borgia Butler."

It was another housing project, across the road from Claremont Village, but Borgia Butler was much more open to a police attack. It didn't have the same feeling of infinite space. "You wouldn't last a month, Dave. You'd have constant power failures. I ought to know. I monkeyed with the generators when I was Commish. We intended to hit Claremont Village through Borgia Butler, but I canceled the strike. Too many civilians would have been clopped in the crossfire."

"Isaac, why tell me now? I'm not your snitch."

"But you could help me, Dave. Richardson has disappeared into the dunes. I'd like to grab the cocksucker."

"But I'm a roofboy, and roofboys are blind to what happens down below."

"Dave, your searchlight can cover half the Bronx. You deal all the time. People talk."

"Not about Richardson."

"Then what about the Shooter, Abner Gumm?"

"That pathetic little guy? I let him take whatever pictures he wants. He's been documenting us, writing a book."

"For the Bronx brigade. He's one of Richardson's rats."

"Isaac, you'd better blow. The lords are getting jealous. They'll shoot out my lights."

Isaac started to leave with Barbarossa, while the warlords sat in their fiberglass vests and saluted him. "El Caballo."

They shoved north to Crotona Park, stopped at the City Register's office on Arthur Avenue, with its own medieval accounting; computers hadn't come this far into the Bronx. The clerks asked Isaac for his autograph. He looked at the borough's property map, block by block, with the little blue tags that recorded the current owner of individual buildings and lots. His hand started to shake. Richardson had a dozen blue tags. The Shooter another four. Birdy Towne had five. There was even a blue tag in Bernardo Dublin's name. Sidereal Ventures was tagged two hundred and eighteen times. None of that worried him until he saw the tags devoted to Marianna Storm. Sixteen of them.

He rushed into the deputy register's rooms. That deputy worked for him. His name was Myron Small. Isaac gathered his own best bag of tricks. "Myron, are you a Democrat?"

"Yes, Mr. Mayor. I'm delighted to—"

"Loyal and true?"

"Yes, Mr. Mayor."

"And if I told you that I was conducting an investigation, you'd keep the news under your hat?"

"Forever," said the deputy. "Or at least as long as I could."

"Can a twelve-year-old girl own property in the Bronx?"

"Strictly speaking? Yes and no. Children, even cats and dogs, can hold title. Your little girl could gobble up half the borough, but she couldn't buy or sell without a guardian behind her."

"So her appearance on a deed is almost like a decoration."

"More than that. Once she comes of age, the property will—"

"Myron, can you tell me who's the president and chief executive officer of Sidereal Ventures?"

"It's in the public record, Mr. Mayor."

"Myron, I'm asking you."

Myron Small scratched about in a huge filing cabinet, returned with a tattered card. "Mr. Mayor, this is a privileged source, and I—"

"Man or woman, Myron?"

"Woman . . . Mrs. J. Michael Storm."

Isaac kissed his deputy on the forehead. "The mayor's like a glass man, isn't he, Myron?"

"I don't—"

"He comes and goes . . . I've never been here, Myron. We never talked. You never opened your filing cabinet for me."

And while the deputy blinked and brooded, Isaac was already out the door.

17

He had so much bitterness, he had to get back into the sky. The chopper landed on a knoll in Crotona Park, and Isaac climbed aboard with Joe. They sat above the Bronx, Isaac imagining a mountain of blue tags. His eyes began to tear from all the rage in him, and he couldn't even look for Alyosha.

It was Joe who got him out of the chopper and brought him home to Marilyn the Wild. She didn't badger the Big Guy. Marilyn could sense his murderous solitude. She rocked him in her arms, the only father she would ever have, and he was almost like a baby. She wished she had milk in her breasts for Isaac the Brave.

She fed him chicken soup, and felt a terrible desire for Joe. It could have been incest. She didn't care what you called it. She would have stripped Joe, sat on him while Isaac watched, but it would only have deepened his solitude.

Marilyn behaved. She combed her father's hair, groomed his magnificent sideburns.

"Dad," she said, "we could stay in the mansion with you . . . or you could stay here."

"Children," he said, "the City never sleeps . . . I have work to do."

But he couldn't move. He had no life in his legs, a glass man from a glass house. He fell asleep on the sofa. Marilyn had to phone the mansion. "Isaac's with us," she growled. "And I don't want him disturbed."

But the calls began to arrive from this deputy mayor and that. Candida Cortez, deputy mayor for finance, screamed something about the Fire Department Pension Fund. Marilyn took it all down. There were at least nine crises at City Hall. Marilyn turned philosophical. She would have roused her dad for one crisis, but nine of them could wait.

"Alyosha," he mumbled in his sleep. Marilyn dozed in a chair beside her dad, got up with him in the middle of the night, gave him a glass of water, went back to sleep, abandoning poor Joe, who lay alone in the bedroom like an exile.

Isaac woke at noon, Marilyn still beside him. They had cornflakes together, fresh strawberries and skim milk. Marilyn made her dad a cappuccino. He was almost content. He showered and shaved under his sideburns with one of Joey's blades.

"Where's the son-in-law?"

"In the Bronx," Marilyn said, "looking for that little artist."

Isaac shoved his Glock inside his pants, pecked Marilyn on the cheek, and strolled up to Sutton Place South. Marianna had gone to her aikido class, but Clarice was at home with her bodyguards, Milton and Sam, who wanted to frisk the Big Guy. He wouldn't let them near his Glock. He pulled it out of his pants, like Jesse James, stuck it between their skulls. "Dismiss them, Clarice. No more bodyguards."

"Are you crazy?" she said. "What about Fantômas?"

"Fantômas is sick . . . he's lying in bed. Get rid of your geeks."

"Who's a geek?" Milton said.

"Sonny, I'm the mayor of New York. I could rip up your license, if you have one. Leave!"

"Clarice?" Sam said.

"Listen to him. He's a maniac. I'll see you later."

"There is no later. If these lads come back, they'll wish they'd never heard of Manhattan."

Milton and Sam slumped out of the apartment. Clarice slapped Isaac, dug at him with her nails. The Glock fell out of his hand. She slapped him again, and Isaac smiled as he tasted his own blood. He couldn't believe how beautiful she was with her nostrils flaring, her gray eyes shining with hostility. His anger fell away.

They started to kiss, and suddenly the Big Guy was rolling in the carpets without his clothes. He hadn't been near another woman ever since Margaret Tolstoy had floated back into his life. He wasn't gentle with Clarice. He caressed her with a certain meanness, and the two of them made love like a couple of warring seals.

"You've been wanting to do this for a long time, haven't you, Isaac? It's like getting back at your old student, the baseball czar. It excites you . . . fucking J. and me at the same time."

"J. wasn't my student. I counseled him when he was at Columbia . . . got him out of a jam."

"Isaac, you know what I mean."

He'd been thinking of Bernardo, not J. Michael Storm. If Bernardo hadn't betrayed him, the Big Guy might not have left his spittle on Clarice. But he wasn't sure who was cuckolding whom. He'd lost his bearings in the carpets, the compass inside his head that seemed to connect him with other people.

He took a bath with Clarice, sat in a tub that was larger than his old living room on Rivington Street, where he'd lived before he inherited the mayor's glass house.

"Isaac, why were you so rough on my bodyguards?"

"Because you don't need them," Isaac said, stepping out of the tub and climbing into his boxer shorts. He had a craving, a terrible tooth, for Marianna's cookies. But he didn't want to steal into the kitchen and abandon Clarice . . . no, he would have abandoned her if he'd had an inkling that Marianna's cookies were there.

"How did it start, Clarice? The business with Sidereal?"

She'd been drying her legs, and Isaac watched her from the mirror, the fluting of her back, the soft, curving skin.

"What are you talking about?"

"Come on, Clarice. Why the sudden philanthropic interest in the Bronx?"

"I've hardly ever been to the Bronx."

"Hardly ever been? That could slide you out of any scrape. Sidereal is very thirsty. It wants to buy the Bronx. And you're its president and CEO."

"It's a technicality, Isaac. I sign a lot of documents that I never read."

"And do you sign for Marianna, Madam President? How are her properties doing, huh?"

"It was J.'s idea," she said, pulling away from Isaac and putting on her blouse. "Don't you understand? We're penniless. I've been living off the equity on our Houston home."

"And this apartment?"

"Window dressing. It belongs to my favorite aunt . . . J. invested in stupid things, spent and spent, and Sidereal was supposed to recoup our losses, get us back on our feet."

"But the Bronx hasn't seen a real-estate boom in forty years."

"J. was going to make his own boom."

"Jesus, how many cities has J. been speculating in?"

"Only one," said Clarice.

"Why not Baltimore and Albuquerque? There have to be other ratlands."

"You know J. He's only interested in the bleakest of the bleak."

"The bleakest of the bleak . . . I'm sorry, my dear. He pinpointed the Bronx because it was so fucking dependent on Yankee Stadium. He's the czar. He could open the stadium or keep it closed. But not even the Yankees can save all that real estate. He's working in tandem, isn't he? With Billy the Kid. What has Billy promised J.?"

"The moon."

"Billy ends the strike with J.'s help, and he waltzes into the White House. That's how popular he'll become. He promises to rebuild the Bronx. Industrial parks on Sidereal sites."

"Something like that."

Isaac started to shake her. "What did you see in my eyes when I got here? That I uncovered your game? And you decided to make a little lovey . . . to quiet the mayor."

Clarice slapped Isaac again and again. He didn't grab her hand. Both sides of his mouth were bleeding. She stopped, started to cry.

"Where's Bernardo? When can I see him?"

"He's convalescing at the mansion . . . one of your partners, Richardson, wanted to wind his clock."

"I don't have any partners."

"Is Richardson the go-between, the guy who brings governors and thieves together?"

"Ask him."

"I would, Clarice. But he's disappeared with the whole Bronx brigade . . . you aren't fighting with J., are you? It's a big act."

"And the shiner he gave me?"

"Window dressing," Isaac said.

"I'm divorcing the son of a bitch, but I can't help it if

my finances are tied to his. If J. goes down, I go down."

"And poor Bernardo. He's your chevalier, the un-clever knight. You suckered him into coming here, into putting on that mask."

"I did not," she said. "I did not. I was frightened . . ."

"So frightened that you made it with him."

"I didn't plan anything, Isaac. I wasn't waiting for Fantômas. But I could feel him hesitate . . . it excited me."

"And would I excite you, Madam President, if I wore a mask?"

"No," she said. "You're not Fantômas."

They didn't even kiss at the door. They weren't strangers or slightly familiar friends, just Merliners caught in some muddle. And the Big Guy had to wonder if he'd made love to a ghost. But this ghost was melancholy. Isaac could read remorse in her gray eyes.

"You won't tell Bernardo, will you?"

"Shouldn't you be thinking of J.?" Isaac said, profoundly jealous.

"I don't give a damn about J."

Finally she did hug Isaac, kissed him between the eyes, and he went down the elevator like a bear who'd just eaten a brick of candy . . . until he bumped into Marianna in the lobby. She was carrying her aikido sword in the same cotton scabbard she would bring to Gracie Mansion. Was Marianna her mother's accom-plice? Another officer of Sidereal Ventures who lent her name to a lot of deeds? And had Merlin become one more conduit for Mr. and Mrs. Storm? Is that why J.

was so eager to join? J. was putting on a show, trying to impress Isaac. The baseball czar was already a secret member of the Merliners . . .

"Hello, Marianna."

She blinked, barely seemed to recognize the Big Guy. Was she counting her fortune?

"Uncle Isaac, you were supposed to bring me a present."

"What present?" he asked.

"Alyosha."

"Barbarossa's on the case."

"Always relying on other people. I'll have to find him myself."

"Don't you dare. It isn't safe in the dunes. There are wild dogs . . . and gangs . . . and rotten policemen. We'll go together. In my chopper. But first I have to—"

"Promises, promises," Marianna said, and she ran into the elevator with her scabbard, leaving Isaac all alone.

18

He showed up on Pine Street, at Porter Endicott's bank. "I have an appointment," he told Porter's private secretary, and she didn't dare challenge the mayor, call him a liar. She muttered into her telephone, smiled, and said, "He'll see you now."

Isaac trudged into the banker's office, which had a green carpet, like Yankee Stadium, and he could almost imagine himself in the middle of a baseball diamond, arriving at some stupendous home plate. Porter Endicott sat behind that home plate, a huge oak desk that must have belonged to one of his great-granduncles.

"Isaac," Porter said, "I'm enchanted to see you, but I'm expecting a call from Switzerland, and I have to prepare my notes."

"I'm talking survival. Switzerland can wait."

"Whose survival?"

"Yours. Mine. Billy the Kid's."

Porter took a tiny tape recorder out of his pocket, turned it on. "Are you threatening me, Your Honor?"

"Put that contraption away. This is strictly off-the-cuff."

"Is that why you rushed down here from City Hall? To tell me my hours and what phone calls I can take?"

"I didn't come from City Hall. I was with Clarice . . . Porter, I'd like you to use your pull to sink a certain corporation."

"I'm not the mayor's Wall Street thug. This bank doesn't *sink* corporations."

"Stop it. Your bank's a barracuda. I read it in *Fortune* magazine. 'No mercy,' that's the Endicott motto. You make and break companies all the time."

"And my next victim?"

"Sidereal Ventures."

Porter started to laugh. He returned the tape recorder to his pocket. "Forgive me, Isaac, I . . ."

"What's so funny?"

"Did you discuss this with Candy Cortez?"

"Why? What's Candida got to do with Sidereal?"

"Your deputy mayor is one of Sidereal's principal investors."

"She's been dumping City gelt into that scam?"

"Of course not. It's all her own . . . you can hardly blame her. She's trying to rebuild the Bronx."

"Yeah, on the bones of the hungry and the dead . . . who told her about Sidereal?"

"I might have. I can't remember."

"Ah, I should have figured. You're J. Michael's Manhattan connection . . ."

"Not at all. Sidereal is much too risky for us. But Candy didn't mind the risks. She was adamant about having a Bronx portfolio. And there wasn't much more than Sidereal that I could suggest."

"You think it will prosper, huh? Gimme a banker's opinion."

"I have no opinion, really . . . I told you. Endicott will move money into the Bronx, but at a much slower pace. We're considering a mini-mall right now."

"On Featherbed Lane?"

"That's one possible site. But we'd prefer not to be in the shadow of the Cross Bronx Express."

"Then you're gonna have a hard time locating your little Shangri-la. Because half the Bronx is under that shadow . . . have you been talking with my people about a tax abatement?"

"Not until we find the site."

"That's grand," Isaac said. "And I suppose you'll have a cineplex and a bowling alley and a maternity shop? . . . something to satisfy the poor."

"We haven't done our marketing yet."

"And how do you market madness and crack pipes, thirteen-year-old mothers, firebugs who aren't even tall enough to sit in a chair?"

"Would you rather we stay out of the Bronx?"

"No. But I still want you to sink Sidereal."

"Isaac, how did the last romantic on earth ever get to be mayor of New York?"

"That's politics. People love a guy who isn't eager to run. I can make an awful stink. I'll tie Billy and J. to kids that Richardson murdered."

"Careful, Isaac. Richardson's a celebrated gangbuster. And those kids are casualties of war."

"Believe what you want. But I don't like it when a prosecutor starts executing children . . . either you sink Sidereal or I sink Billy the Kid."

Isaac ran out of the bank, phoned Candida Cortez from a cigar store, shouted at her. She was the mayor's prodigy. A daughter of the Bronx who'd graduated from Barnard and the Wharton School of Business. Isaac had nursed her along when he was Commish, had put her in charge of management and budget at the NYPD, and moved her to his own table when he inherited his glass house. She was the youngest deputy mayor in the Sidel administration.

"I want you to sell all your holdings in Sidereal. Candy . . ."

"Boss, we'd better meet."

He walked over to Ratner's. Candida was already there, at one of the back booths. The waiters wouldn't stop pestering Isaac. He had to scratch his signature on countless slips of paper. Candida had one white hair. She was thirty-two. She wasn't as volatile as Marilyn the Wild, but she was almost as precious to him. They feasted on onion rolls, cups of black coffee, and apple strudel.

"You'll sell," Isaac said.

"I won't."

"Candy, I'll fry your ass. I'll make you into a clerk."

"You couldn't, grandpa. You'd only start to cry."

"I don't understand. You're the sharpest money manager I've ever seen. Wasn't there a prospectus?"

"Yes, and I prepared it."

"Shh," Isaac said. "You wouldn't stab me like that. Richardson's a snake."

"You used to love him, Isaac. You talked about him all the time, pulled him out of the Bronx district attorney's office to run your brigade. Didn't Brock find Alyosha for you?"

"He's still a snake."

"I'm sleeping with him," Candida said.

Isaac started to choke on the strudel. Candida had to reach around and pat him on the back. "My doctor thinks I'm pregnant."

"It isn't fair. How can I waste him if you're carrying his child?"

"*Our* child," she said.

"He can't face me. He's disappeared into the dunes."

"That's because he's fond of you, Isaac. And he doesn't want to kill you."

"Kill me? You can't kill a mayor."

"You can in the Bronx. Didn't you say the Bronx has its own weather? Anything can happen."

"I lived there with Marilyn. In Riverdale."

"Riverdale isn't the Bronx, Isaac. It's a golden tooth at the edge of the map. You didn't have to fall asleep to a hundred different fires, or keep wild dogs out of your pants. That's why I bought into Sidereal."

"Sidereal's gonna save the Bronx, huh?"

"I never said that. But at least it will keep out the vultures and encourage local people to invest."

"Like Mr. and Mrs. J. Michael Storm."

"We had to bring in J. I couldn't be on the board of

directors. Did you want me to deal for Sidereal *and* City Hall?"

"God forbid. But did you know that Prince Martin Lima is backing J.? The biggest dope dealer in the Bronx."

"Then we'll have to do dope to stay alive. I don't mess with J."

Isaac grabbed an onion roll. His choking fit was gone. "Well, somebody will have to . . . he can't rule the Bronx just because he's the baseball czar and Yankee Stadium is beholden to him."

"But that's the problem, Isaac. He does rule the Bronx. Nobody else but J. can solve that baseball war. Without him the borough's asleep."

"Where can I find Richardson?"

"He'll find you."

She got up, grabbed the check, paid for Isaac's strudel at the counter, touched her white hair, and fled from Ratner's. Isaac finished his coffee, signed a few more slips, and marched into the street, but he couldn't seem to shake all his admirers. Milton and Sam were waiting for him. Clarice's bodyguards. And the Big Guy was almost glad. He couldn't wait to toss the two of them on their ass.

But Milton and Sam were much more agile away from Clarice. They seized Isaac by his pants, spun him around, and tossed him into a blue Cadillac, where a mousy little woman attended to him. Milton held his arms while the woman painted Isaac's face with a fat brush. Were they preparing him for the undertaker? He tried to struggle, and Sam hit him so hard that Isaac's whole body whipped across the Cadillac and his ears started to ring. Sam hit him again. *It isn't fair,* Isaac muttered to himself and fell into a tiny coma.

19

The Big Guy woke in some kind of dressing room. He had a white napkin hanging from his neck. There were make-up artists all over him, handling him roughly. "Two minutes," they mumbled. "His forehead is still shiny . . . and what about the gray hairs in his nose . . . he looks like shit."

They attacked his sideburns, plucked the gray hairs from his nose, and Isaac felt like a disappointed diva. He'd been in the same hot seat before. It was two minutes to airtime, and there was the typical pandemonium. Milton was picking his nails. Sam was laughing to himself. They adjusted Isaac's Glock inside his pants.

"Who are you guys?"

"We work for Billy the Kid," Sam said. "And Billy asked us to watch over Clarice."

They belonged to the Gov's elite squad of commandoes. They traveled with him around the country, functioned like a secret service.

"You're protecting her from Fantômas, I suppose."

"Sure," Sam said. "If this Fantômas happens to be J. Michael Storm."

"But why would Billy interfere? He's picked J. as his running mate. They're practically married."

Milton winked at Isaac. "Maybe it isn't the Gov's idea of marriage."

"Please," the make-up artists said, "we have thirty seconds."

"Keep quiet," Sam said, and the two commandoes plucked off the napkin, pulled Isaac out of his seat, led him across a labyrinth of cables and into a studio where J. Michael sat with Billy the Kid in luxurious armchairs, next to Wooster Freeman, host of *Wooster, Dead or Alive*, the nation's most popular afternoon talk show. Isaac could recognize Tim Seligman in the audience, with other Democrats, under the low-key lights; Wooster was an ex-war correspondent who liked to spar with celebrities. But he'd always been easy on Isaac.

"Welcome to our mystery guest," he shouted into the cameras. "Sidel, who serves this City twenty-five hours a day. You see him up in the sky, watching the five boroughs, relentless champion of anything and everything New York."

The audience whistled and yelled, "We want Isaac," until Wooster quieted them with a single clap. Isaac shook hands with Billy and J. and sat down in his own armchair. Wooster motioned to Billy the Kid.

"We have some excitement in the air, wouldn't you say, Governor?"

"I couldn't promise," Billy said, displaying his aquiline nose to the cameras, the depth of his blue eyes. "But you know how much the baseball strike has hurt us. And I can't afford to let this happen, not while I'm governor. We've been putting pressure on the clubs, getting them to realize how vital the game is to all of us. New Yorkers are the ones who are suffering the most. We have a special claim, don't we, Mr. Mayor?"

Who was rehearsing that cocksucker? Who was feeding him his lines? J. Michael Storm. "Yes," Isaac muttered, "we do have a claim."

"Baseball wasn't invented in Cooperstown," Billy said. "That's an old wives' tale. Organized baseball was born in Manhattan. The very first club was the New York Knickerbockers . . ."

"Hardly," Isaac said. "It was the Bronx Bachelors, made up of volunteer firemen, guys who lived in boardinghouses and loved to play ball. The team captain was Rupert Manly, who organized matches with the Knickerbockers on a hill in Hoboken called the Elysian Fields."

"Ah, a touch of heaven and hell," Billy said. "Isaac is never wrong."

"I'm not so sure," said J. Michael Storm. "Did Manly have his own rulebook?"

"He didn't need rulebooks. He kept all the rules in his head."

Wooster Freeman plunged right into the argument.

"Is Michael trying to tell us that the Bronx Bachelors are a figment of your imagination, Mr. Mayor?"

"Figment, eh? Walt Whitman saw them play in 1846. 'Their game was glorious,' he said, after watching the Bachelors cream Manhattan."

"Wooster," said Billy the Kid, "we're bringing back baseball. We have to win the war."

Wooster smiled at Sidel. "And what do you think, Mr. Mayor?"

"If we can't get the Yankees, I'll have to recall the Bachelors from their grave."

"And I'll have to lock them out of Yankee Stadium," said J. Michael Storm. "We won't tolerate scabs."

"J.," Isaac said, "how can anyone grant an injunction against a team of ghosts?"

"Ghosts have no special privileges," said J. Michael Storm. "They can go down in a court of law . . . it's the Yankees, or nothing."

Isaac began to feel nauseous. Billy the Kid was running for president on *Wooster, Dead or Alive*. And J. Michael was his battery mate. But why the hell had Billy's commandoes copped Isaac and delivered him to Wooster's show? Was it to sanctify Billy's marriage to J. and serve as justice of the peace? J. sulked for most of the hour, while Billy recited little homilies he must have memorized for weeks. The Gov was preparing his presidential face . . .

Isaac cornered J. Michael after Billy left the studio. J. continued to sulk. "The Gov's giving it to me in the ass."

"Billy's a real heartbreaker, but I thought he was being nice."

"Nice? He says if I can't end the strike in forty-eight hours, he'll go after Clarice."

"That's funny," Isaac said. "His own special cops have been protecting Clarice from you."

"Clarice doesn't need protection."

"Didn't you bang her up a bit?"

"Isaac, that woman tried to stab me with a knife."

"Was it a lovers' quarrel, or something to do with Sidereal?"

They both sat in the dressing room, glancing into the mirror with powder on their cheeks: they could have been ghostly players on Isaac's team, the Bachelors of the Bronx.

"Isaac, am I gonna get shit from you about a company that's dropping into the ground?"

"That's not how Porter sees it. He says Sidereal is a dream . . . and you're a liar, J. You did try to loop Clarice. You asked Brock Richardson to send an Apache after her, that man in the mask."

"Fantômas?"

"No. Bernardo Dublin, her chevalier."

"I had to freak her out. She was threatening to seize my shares in Sidereal if I didn't keep away from her and Marianna."

"What if Brock had sent the wrong Apache, someone who broke her neck?"

"Come on, Bernardo was tailor-made for the job. He wouldn't have whacked Clarice."

"But you couldn't have known that. You wanted her dead, or something close. Like a docile wife in a wheelchair. You were counting on it. And when it didn't happen, you flipped your tactics around, used Bernardo to your own fucking advantage."

"Didn't you call him her chevalier? Well, she's had other chevaliers, including Billy the Kid."

"Billy's been boffing your wife?"

"And so have you . . . I'm still her husband. Clarice tells me everything. And don't think I'm crushed. She says you're the lousiest lay she ever had, next to Billy. But at least she's fond of you. Billy's an icicle."

Isaac rose out of his chair, seized J. Michael by the collar, and started to twist. "You've been choreographing her lovelife, haven't you, J.? Like a pious little general. Billy sleeps with Clarice, and he doesn't even blink while you and Richardson and your lousy client, Prince Martin Lima, rape the Bronx."

"Lima isn't my client."

"Yeah," Isaac said, ripping J.'s collar right off his shirt. "And Snow White never laid eyes on the Seven Dwarfs . . . I'm Isaac, remember? You don't have to play innocent with me. You're the prince's man in Texas and the Bronx. You launder money for that little son of a bitch. And Sidereal is your personal laundry room. I ought to strangle you, J., but there's only one baseball czar. And he's immortal until the lights go on at Yankee Stadium."

The Big Guy wiped off the powder and paint, but J. Michael pawed at him. "Isaac, don't leave me here."

"You're untouchable. You're on top of the world."

"Billy doesn't think so. He'd like to damage me."

"And lose his running mate?"

"He'd prefer a vice-president without a pair of balls."

"You can always decide not to run."

"It's too late. I've already promised myself to Seligman. He controls all the Party patronage. He could have me drummed out of my own firm."

"Then I'll light a candle, J., and cry for you."

Isaac strolled into the corridor, but the baseball czar clung to him. Wooster stood in the semidarkness with Tim Seligman, smoking Cuban cigars. Isaac watched the burning ash next to their teeth.

"Tim, was it your idea to make me Wooster's mystery man?"

"A little national exposure can't hurt," Seligman said. "I wanted the Gov to bask in your glory. It's important. I'd like the public to regard you, Billy, and J. as our Three Musketeers."

"But isn't that one musketeer too many? You can't have two vice-presidents on the same ticket."

"Ah, but we'll manage, won't we, Wooster?"

"Of course," Wooster said. "What other city can boast a law and order liberal, a radical cop?"

"I'm not a cop anymore. That's what people keep telling me."

"But you'll always be our Pink Commish," Wooster said. "Isn't that true, J.?"

J. crept out from behind Isaac's shoulder. "Yes," he said.

"J.'s been a bad boy," Seligman said. "He's sort of blackmailing us. Can't make up his mind to end the strike."

"Tim, I have owners and players to contend with."

"That isn't our problem, not while Billy is stagnating

in all the polls. He needs some thunder and lightning. And you're our thunder god, our Zeus . . . knock some sense into him, will you, Isaac?"

"I'll try," Isaac said, dancing into the street like a good Democrat, J. just behind him. Milton and Sam stood in front of their blue Cadillac, eating enormous ice-cream cones covered with specks of chocolate.

"Your Honor," Sam said, "you can go home . . . but we have some business with Mr. Storm. Ask him to get into the car."

"Couldn't do that, lads," Isaac said, adopting his policeman's brogue, a melody he'd learned from a long line of Irish cops. Billy's henchmen shouldn't have come at Isaac eating ice-cream cones. He shoved the cones into their muzzles, confused them, made their eyes start to water, then banged their heads together, and shouted at the baseball czar, "Start running, huh? I can't do this all day."

"But where should I go?"

"To Houston and Chicago, J. And settle that strike if you want to keep alive."

The baseball czar darted across the street, while Milton reached for his Glock. Isaac kicked the gun out of Milton's hand, pivoted like a toreador, punched Milton and Sam into the ground. People began to gather, but they didn't seem alarmed: they liked to catch their mayor in the middle of a brawl. He was their favorite hooligan, and they would have gladly helped him out. But the Big Guy wasn't looking for help. All his anger seemed to descend on Milton and Sam, his hatred of politics, his disgust with Sidereal, a corporation with all the tentacles and inky blood of an octopus. He was one lone hombre, El Caballo, stuck in a war he could no longer grasp. He pummeled Milton and Sam, who couldn't fight a mayor surrounded by all his fans. Then he looked up, saw Wooster and Tim Seligman outside the studio, cheering Isaac. The further he ran from politics, the deeper he was enmeshed. "Alyosha," he muttered, longing for the dunes. He'd have to disappear, suck his own thumbs and pray that no one nominated him for anything. El Caballo.

Part Five

20

—*H*ey, *marica, maricón.*

Alyosha would find little caves in the Park Avenue trestle and live like a rat, surviving on old candy bars and containers of sour milk. The Malay Warriors and the San Juan Freaks had given up the chase. They couldn't track Alyosha and avoid Richardson's Apaches, who were following them as they followed the kid, and picking them off two and three at a time. But it was Alyosha's own gang, the Jokers, who persisted, with certain Dixie Cups, borrowed from the Dominoes. They would howl at Alyosha, call him a cunt in their own Bronx vocabulary.

—*Hey, fruta bomba, how are you, man?*

He might have surrendered to the Jokers, but not to the Dixie Cups, who sucked on their pipes and sold crack to infants while they pursued Alyosha.

—*Hey, marica, maricón, did you know that Paulie's dead?*

Paul was a magician, like the Big Jew. You couldn't kill Paul. But Alyosha got suspicious. Why would the Jokers and the Dixie Cups keep singing that same little song?

—*Fruta bomba, Paulie's dead 'cause of you.*

He took a quarter out of his pocket, raced into a telephone booth near the trestle, dialed Rikers, haggled with the operator, who finally switched his call to the max security center, where a guard got on the line and teased Alyosha.

"Paulito aint registered at our hotel."

"But where is he?"

"Try the Atlantic Ocean . . . or the Bronx morgue."

And the phone went dead before Alyosha could say another word. He didn't have a fresh coin to shove into the slot, and he shouldn't have exposed himself. Because there could have been a stray Freak who hadn't given up the hunt and was looking for a little reward money. But the coast was clear, and Alyosha ran beside the tracks, wondering if he should hurl rocks at a passing train, but it wouldn't have given him pleasure to harm any of the ricos who lived in Connecticut, where Alyosha had never been. He could duck into the shadows, but he couldn't escape the voices around him.

—*Fruta bomba, fruta bomba, who murdered Paul?*

Alyosha started to shiver, because all the maricónes couldn't have had the same theme unless some of it was true. He was hungry for cash. He had to have another quarter. He put on his blue handkerchief, wore it like a mask, waited outside a grocery store and stopped a niño who couldn't have been more than five.

"Homey," he shouted under the muslin of his mask, "gimme all you got."

The niño started to cry. "Mamá will kill me."

"Hey, you're talking to Angel Carpenteros. Why should I care?"

But as he grabbed the niño's grocery bag and little black purse that must have been swollen with coins, he suffered a knock on his wrist, a savage blow that could have come from a hammer or one of Richardson's blackjacks. He dropped the groceries and the purse.

The niño didn't have the courage to scoop them up and run. He stood like a frozen article, a baby antelope at the Bronx Zoo, while Alyosha looked into the eyes of his enemy. It was Marianna Storm, clutching a wooden sword. His own little Grushenka had hacked at his hand.

"Alyosha," she said, "let the boy go."

"I aint stopping him . . . homey, get the hell out of here."

"Mamá," the niño said, then bowed to Marianna Storm and sidled past her with all his stuff.

"Take off that idiotic mask," she said.

"It's not so idiotic. My brother gave it to me . . . it belongs to his gang."

"Well, I've had enough of masks, thank you."

Alyosha removed the handkerchief mask and put it into his pocket. He kept staring at the sword. It was the hottest item he'd ever seen in the Bronx. A wooden sword tall as Marianna herself.

"Where'd you get the blade?"

"From my aikido class."

Aikido hadn't come to El Bronx, the home of Latin kung fu, where a kick in the groin was worth a hundred guns and knives. But Alyosha wasn't much of a street fighter. He could only mark up walls.

"Marianna, I could use a quarter."

"My hero, who robs groceries from little boys."

"I was desperate. I'm looking for a piece of news, and I can't find it without the telephone."

"I never carry money. It's useless. I wouldn't be caught dead with a lot of nickels and dimes in my pocket. Money weighs you down."

The chica was crazy, talking Manhattan near the Park Avenue trestle. "Then how did you get up here? Did you flap your wings or fly in Uncle Isaac's iron bird?"

"I took a cab," she said, "charged the ride to American Express."

"Then your driver must have been a dummy. Because no one takes plastic in the Bronx . . . all the Jokers use plastic as playing cards."

"But I still found you, Alyosha, thanks to American Express."

"It wasn't American Express. I came out of my hole to hunt for coins . . . and if you hadn't stopped me, I would have made my call."

"Silly," she said. "It's the easiest thing in the world to utilize the telephone."

She crawled into the nearest booth with Alyosha, asked him for the number he wanted, sweet-talked the operator into dialing it for her, and charged the call to Clarice. And Alyosha got on the line with Gloria Guralnik, Richardson's humpbacked secretary. "Gloria," he said, "it's me. Has Richardson gone to any funerals lately?"

"None that I know of."

Then Paulito had to be alive. But there was a jerkiness in Gloria's voice, like she was a girl who wanted to cry but couldn't, because she'd been around Apaches too long and had lived with their cruelties. "Alyosha, you have my deepest sympathies."

"Sympathies for what?"

"Paulito. He strangled himself. That's what Brock says."

Alyosha knew about such strangulations. It was an old Apache trick. "But when's the funeral?"

"There isn't any. Paul is lying in some icebox, while the police do their reports . . . Richardson's in the field. I'll beep him for you."

And before Alyosha could hang up, he heard Richardson's voice. "Homey, is that you?"

"You bitch, you did Paul."

"Had to, homey. He was embarrassing me. I kept him alive in the hole. And our agreement was that he'd stay there, and I wouldn't have to ruin his gang completely. But the fool borrows money from Martin Lima and walks right out of Rikers."

"But it's your fault, Richardson. You let the world

know that I was one of your rats, and Paulie had to come looking for me . . ."

"And face his own funeral."

"That's the problem, Richardson. My brother can't even get into the ground."

"It'll happen, homey. I'll see to it. I'm just a soldier. I can't order him out of that icebox, but I'll take you to him. It's the least I can do."

"No," Alyosha said. "I'll blind you, Richardson, I'll do worse."

"Ah, I thought we were friends. Didn't I encourage your art and introduce you to the Big Guy and little Marianna with the titties? Tell me where you are, homey, and I'll bring you in."

"You'll never find me. And don't turn your back to the wind. Because I'll be there, Richardson, I'll be there."

Alyosha rushed out of that glass booth with Marianna Storm. He'd have to go underground, crawl into the trestle and keep to the caves until he could steal a Glock or jump on Richardson with a hot needle. But he couldn't even get five feet from the booth. Richardson appeared with a couple of Apaches, including Birdy Towne. They all had field radios in their pockets.

Brock whistled at Marianna's wooden sword and pecked her on the hand. He was wearing his cowboy boots and mustard-colored pants.

"How are you, Miz Marianna?"

"Don't talk to him," Alyosha said. "He killed my brother and he'll kill us."

"How's J. Michael's only daughter? I hear Billy the Kid's in love with you."

"Who's Billy the Kid?" Alyosha had to ask, curious and jealous at the same time.

"The next goddamn president of the United States."

"Is he part of your gang?"

All the Apaches started to laugh. "If he aint," Birdy said, "he will be."

"Watch your mouth," Richardson said. "You don't want to give Miz Marianna grandiose notions about ourselves. We're soldiers in the field. We don't do politics."

"But whose soldiers are you?" Marianna asked.

"Darling," Birdy said, "we belong to the City of New York."

"Uncle Isaac doesn't think so. He says you're outlaws, dealing for yourselves."

"Well, you just ask your daddy about that . . . we're a bunch of altruists, trying to build a better Bronx. And we don't need the Big Guy. Our mandate is from Billy the Kid."

"Birdy," Richardson said, "didn't I tell you to watch your mouth? You'll confuse the little girl."

"It's not so confusing," Alyosha said. "I was never out of your sight, not for a minute. You worked me like a magnet. When the Malay Warriors and the Freaks got close, you grabbed them off the street."

"It's like Birdy says. We're building a better Bronx . . . I'll take you to your brother."

Richardson rasped into his radio, "The falcon's on the ground, the falcon's on the ground." Three mustard-colored Fords arrived, and Richardson invited Alyosha and Marianna Storm into the first car.

"We're not going," Alyosha said. "It's a trap. You'll glock us once we get in."

"Homey," Richardson said. "I could glock you right here. No one's listening. There aren't any echoes in the Bronx."

"Good. But at least I won't have to die with the stink of marijuana in my nose."

"You hurt my feelings, homey. I enjoy lighting up with all my rats."

He shoved Alyosha into the mustard-colored car. Marianna followed him inside. She could barely breathe. Richardson's car was like an opium den. Alyosha whispered in her ear. "Did the Big Guy really say Richardson's an outlaw?"

"No," she whispered back. "I made it up. But I wasn't wrong."

The three cars drove away from the railroad tracks, with their sirens on, Alyosha sitting next to Birdy Towne, Richardson's very own strangler. Marianna sat with the sword between her legs. None of the Apaches had even considered disarming her. She wasn't Fordham Road and Featherbed Lane. She was a little rich girl from beyond the pale, who was now the property of the Bronx brigade, one more piece of body armor Richardson had collected to counter the Big Guy. Isaac couldn't survive without Marianna's cookies . . .

The mustard-colored Fords reached Bronx Municipal Hospital, and Birdy pinned on his gold shield and escorted Alyosha into the county morgue. The assistant coroners treated Birdy like their own little brother. They fed him sandwiches, borrowed some of his stash to bake a marijuana meat loaf, drank slivovitz with him, while Alyosha sat with Paulie, who was in a metal case. Paul had marks on his neck, where the Apaches must have strangled him, because Birdy couldn't have done Paulito on his own. And it was sort of insane. Paulito looked alive. Alyosha kept expecting him to say something, to curse the Apaches and Alyosha himself for betraying the Jokers to a brigade of thugs who weren't even noble enough to merit the colors of a Bronx gang.

"Paulie," Alyosha said, "I didn't . . ."

Birdy pranced next to Alyosha with his cup of slivovitz. "Hey, you talking to the dead?"

"He's got a soul, like David Six Fingers."

"David's dead, Paulie's dead . . ."

"And there are no more gangs, just Dixie Cups who come from across the river with Martin Lima's merchandise."

"The best little fucking salesmen in the world."

"And their clients are one step out of kindergarten."

"It's the Bronx, man. Anything goes. Didn't Richardson turn you into a millionaire?"

"Sorry to disappoint you," Alyosha said. "My brushes and rags and spray cans chewed up all the blood money I ever got."

Birdy pushed the refrigerated box back into the wall, and Alyosha lost Paulito again. He was heartsore. What was the point of having a cappuccino machine if he could never share it with Paul? Birdy led him out of the morgue and into the hospital cafeteria, where Richardson's men had captured their own table. Marianna sat beside them, eating a salad with a plastic knife and fork, while the Apaches stared at her artistry. Only Richardson himself could wield a knife and fork like that. They had to eat on the run, always looking behind them, gobbling food with their hands. Brock had gone to make a couple of phone calls. He was constantly calling people. Princes, governors, baseball czars . . .

"Lemme see that sword," Birdy said, the slivovitz slowing his speech. He took Marianna's sword out of the scabbard, whirled it over his head. But he couldn't seem to find any rhythm. He clutched it like a baseball bat.

"Birdy," Alyosha said, "is Richardson having a telephone conference with his other pirates?"

"Probably."

"Is he going to sell us to Martin Lima?"

"Not Marianna. No way. We've never had our own cookie baker."

"And what about me?"

"You'll sweep the floor . . . and keep her company. The governor's gonna give us a medal, I think. And then we might consider selling the darling to her dad. But you don't have much of a future, little man. We could exhibit you in a cage as the last Latin Joker. Or let you draw your own mural. 'Angel Carpenteros, known as Alyosha, Registered Rat. Rest in Peace, Homey. Paid for by Birdy Towne and the Bronx Brigade' . . ."

Marianna put down her knife and fork. "I'll show you," she said.

Birdy stared at her through the slivovitz that seemed to have settled in the pockets under his eyes. "What?"

"I'll show you." She took the sword out of his hands, swayed at the hips, and shattered Birdy's kneecap with one flawless, fluid line. He howled and sank to the floor. The other Apaches rose up from the table and Marianna tapped their Adam's apples, as if she were initiating them into some Bronx knighthood. They clutched their throats and fell out of their chairs.

"Come," Marianna said, grabbing Alyosha's hand. They ran out of the cafeteria, past two security guards, and onto a crooked street called Seminole Avenue. Alyosha had never been to this part of the Bronx. It was like its own Indian country. He had to chart their route. He chose Choctaw Place. They ran deeper and deeper into Indian country, and Alyosha had no idea where he was. It distressed him. He'd lived under the illusion that he could master any neighborhood, and now he realized for the first time that there was a borough beyond all his expectations, that he wasn't a voyager at all, only a hermit who inhabited Mt. Eden Avenue, and had placed his murals in lonely, isolated spots, and how could he immortalize Paulie, record him forever on some great enormous mother of a wall?

21

The City had its own clockwork, with or without Isaac Sidel. Nicholas Bright, first deputy mayor, didn't have to sit in Isaac's chair. He operated out of a cubbyhole that had once been the mayor's broom closet at City Hall. He would confer with Candida Cortez, move billions of dollars around in his head. It was Candida who was afraid, who needed a palpable Sidel. "Nick, what if we goof?"

"Candy, the mayor's rotten in math. He doesn't even know long division. He can't help us."

"But I wish he wouldn't disappear like that."

Candy Cortez had her own dilemma. Brock Richardson was camping out at her penthouse on the Grand Concourse. It was an apartment that Brock himself had refurbished with Sidereal funds. Candida had six rooms and three baths in an Art Deco palace that had risen out of the ruins. She could play badminton on her terrace and watch the complicated crystal world of the

Chrysler Building. She slept with Brock, but she wouldn't spy on Isaac for him. She was two months pregnant, and she tried to imagine the father Brock might be. Could she ever settle in with that chief of the Bronx Apaches?

She didn't get home until midnight, and she hadn't seen Brock or heard from him in several days. He never called. He would arrive alone, or with his Apaches, and they'd roost on the terrace in their mustard-colored pants, roast a chicken on Candida's grill, drink her wine, smoke grass until their eyes were bloodshot, and then Brock would disappear into the bedroom and crawl on top of her, ride Candida in the dark, and she'd have to beg him to take off his Glock. But he wasn't like the other guerreros she knew. He had his gentle ways under all that mustard-colored camouflage.

She could sniff the marijuana when she got to the door. And it pleased Candida that her own guerrero was waiting for her, that he'd come to the apartment before she did. But he'd brought his Apaches and he was in a foul mood. The meanest of them, Birdy Towne, stood in his underwear, with a plastic kneecap covering his own knee, like a football player might wear.

"Hey, boss," Birdy said, "tell your fox what happened."

"Nothing happened," Richardson said. "You let two fucking infants escape from you and smash your knee."

"But it was one of them magic swords . . ."

"Magic, Birdy? I'd call it a pip-squeak practitioner of martial arts . . . now shut up and show off your new knee to somebody else. Candida's been working like a dog for Uncle Isaac. How is the Big Guy, dear?"

"Nobody knows," Candida said. "He's vanished again."

"That's his nature," Richardson said. "Always hanging out on the rim. The Big Guy is eternally alone."

Richardson shoved past Birdy and the other Apaches, who were lying on Candida's carpet with their roaches, watching reruns of *Miami Vice*, and he followed Candida out onto the terrace. He didn't have a roach in his mouth. He leaned over the railing, into the lights of Manhattan.

"Candy, you ought to charge admission with a view like that. I mean, you can't really do Manhattan, conjure up the skyline, until you're in the Bronx."

"Brock, what's wrong?"

"Wrong?" he said. "I'll need six hundred dollars, dear. I'm short on currency at the moment. A guy can have a million in assets, be the lord of almost everything that's around this roof, and can't even afford a new pair of pants."

"I'll give you the six hundred, Brock, but what about your paycheck?"

"It's garnisheed, the whole damn thing. I have more creditors than Beau Brummell."

"Who's Beau Brummell?"

"Some lord who lived around princes and thought he owned the world. Half of England dressed like

Beau Brummell. He died in an insane asylum without a penny . . . or a proper coat."

"But you could stay with me, Brock. I'll feed you."

"And will you feed my army, dear?"

Candida laughed. "A band of Apaches with garnisheed paychecks?"

"Worse," Richardson said. "They sank all their money into my corporation. Can't even afford a pinch of grass. They've been robbing people, just to stay alive."

"And your Apaches are supposed to protect the Bronx."

"Have you had one burglary in this building? Name me one."

Candida heard the crackle of a field radio. She couldn't comprehend the language. Something about a falcon, a falcon in flight. Birdy had hopped out onto the terrace with his extra kneecap. "Hiya, Miz Candy," he said, clutching his radio. "Boss, do you want to speak to the son-in-law?"

"Shut your mouth," Richardson said.

"Dave says—"

"I don't care what Dave says."

"Well, I aint the falcon. If Barbarossa—"

Richardson tossed an ashtray at Birdy. It spun over Birdy's head and sailed off the roof, into the dead of the Bronx, on the dark side of the terrace. Birdy smiled and hopped back into the living room, and Richardson wondered if he'd have to strangle his sweetheart. Birdy shouldn't have mentioned Barbarossa. Candy was devoted to the Big Guy, Candy might give all of them away.

"I'm pregnant," she said, and Richardson didn't even have to blink. He had her now. She was one more piece of his body armor. "Well, we'll name him Isaac if it's a boy . . . after the Big Guy."

"You're not sorry . . . you don't think I tricked you, Brock?"

"Or Sophie if she's a girl . . . after Isaac's mom. Did you know that she was kicked to death? A gang of young hoods did Sophie Sidel. That's why we have to get tough out on the street. Or the wild dogs will return, and nobody will want to live in the Bronx."

"But we'll have our baby here . . ."

"In the heartland. Didn't I find you six rooms? Who ripped out all the old pipes? Daddy Brock."

"What happened to Barbarossa?"

The bitch was too clever for him. Isaac's own accountant. She did all of the Big Guy's books. "We won't hurt him . . . I promise. But I had to grab the pest, take him off the street. He was trampling in our yard, like a mad dog. And now I can bargain with the Big Guy, keep him off our ass . . . until the baseball war is over. Then we'll all be guzzling pink champagne, and Isaac will have a godson."

"You'll have to give back Barbarossa."

"I will," Richardson said. "Cross my heart." He would strangle her even if she was carrying baby Isaac. But Richardson had a fucking thing about infanticide, particularly when the infant wasn't even born. He was an assistant D.A., a doctor of laws, an academician who'd once taught alongside Isaac at the Police Academy, like some Renaissance man. The Big Guy should have left him alone. Richardson was smoking grass in the county courthouse, minding his own business as the D.A.'s white knight who put all the scumbags away, when Isaac kidnapped him, put him in charge of the Bronx brigade, bought him his first Glock.

Candy kissed him on the cheek. "I'm counting on you, Brock." And at half past midnight she marched off the terrace and into her bath, while Richardson stood near the sky, planning his war against Sidel. He'd pick up Marianna again, dismantle her sword, hold the Big Guy at bay, drown him in a million problems and wait for Billy the Kid. He might even run for congress. There would be books about Brock Richardson, the singular prosecutor who solved urban blight.

"Falcon . . ."

Birdy had sneaked up on him.

"Moron, did you have to mention Barbarossa in front of my bitch?"

"Well, there's a crisis. Barbarossa won't sit still. And Dave—"

"Dave can carve him up."

"What about the Big Guy? I can't do him until I have a whole knee."

"That dinosaur? He can't even remember his own name."

But Brock would have to get rid of Birdy soon, distance himself from his own little reign of terror, scatter all the Apaches. He was waiting for Billy the Kid.

"Boss, there was a brat at the door, a messenger boy. He brung this note, wouldn't even say who it was from."

Richardson snatched at the sheet of brown paper, opened it, smiled at the telltale words. MICKEY MAN- TLE. He tore up the paper, let the bits fly into the wind, danced off the terrace, stole into the bath where Candida lay in the light of a blue candle, climbed into the tub with all his clothes on, and licked her body with more devotion than she'd ever met in Brock.

22

Isaac was in his chopper, watching the news. It was four A.M. J. Michael Storm, the players' czar, had come to terms with the owners' entire negotiation team. He'd defeated the whole idea of a salary cap, demanded and got a minimum wage. The clubs had capitulated to him. "It's a happy day," he told reporters. "Gentlemen, I'm tired. We've been fighting cheek to cheek." He'd been locked in a room at the Mark Hopkins Hotel for eighteen hours, J. Michael and a team of the hardest hitters the owners could find, lawyers who should have eaten J. alive. But they couldn't rankle the czar. He had stubble on his chin when he emerged from the room. His collar was wrinkled. But it was the other lawyers who had long, haggard faces, not the czar.

Isaac caught J.'s act on his miniature screen. He couldn't explain his own feeling of dread. It was almost dawn when he returned to his glass house. He met Clarice coming down the stairs.

"A nocturnal visit, eh?"

"I had to see Bernardo, and nobody could get in touch with you."

"Congratulations. J. ended the war. And you'll be our new second lady, the first one to ever sleep with a president *and* his running mate."

Clarice walloped Isaac, and he twisted about on the stairs, almost fell, like some forlorn acrobat. But the Big Guy regained his footing, grabbed Clarice by the scruff of her neck, and dragged her back upstairs to Bernardo's bedroom.

"Bernardo," Isaac shouted, "I have a present. The royal concubine. Did you know that Clarice has been romancing Billy the Kid?"

But Bernardo wasn't in bed. And Isaac felt a thump on his shoulder, as if some rabid monkey had climbed aboard, and he had to hurl that monkey off his back. It was Bernardo who'd hopped on Isaac from a chair but had exhausted all his energy. He lay on the floor, his bruised face like a black mask. "Fantômas," Isaac muttered.

"She had to sleep with the Gov," Bernardo said. "She was doing it for J., to get him on the Democratic ticket . . . Billy was blackmailing her, said he'd lock her out of Sidereal, bring a special prosecutor down from Albany, and close the entire shop . . . I forgive her."

"And why did she sleep with Sidel?" Isaac almost had to beg.

"Because you're a pitiful son of a bitch with baggy pants," Clarice said.

"Boss, she was protecting me. She thought you

might take away my shield, because of what I was doing in the Bronx . . . I told her everything."

"What happens now, children? J. kicked ass, humbled every baseball owner . . ."

"It was on the radio," Bernardo said from the floor. Isaac took him in his arms, carried him to his quilt.

"That doesn't change anything," Clarice said. "I can't divorce the bastard. I'll play the candidate's wife . . . but I'm not giving up Bernardo."

There was a tap on Isaac's shoulder. He started to howl, turned around, recognized Harvey, his valet.

"I'm having an important conversation, Harve. Life and death. Did you have to interrupt?"

"It's Marilyn, Your Honor. She's been calling all night. She's on line six . . ."

Isaac picked up the phone. His hand was shaking.

"Isaac," his daughter said. "If you wanted to hide so much, you should have sent me Joe."

"Marilyn, I . . ."

"He's been missing for two days . . . something's bad. He never goes to bed without me. Find him, Dad. You're responsible. He's out on one of your suicide patrols."

She hung up on Isaac the Brave.

"What's the matter, boss?" Bernardo asked from under his quilt.

"Barbarossa didn't get back from the Bronx."

"Apaches . . . lemme come with you. I know all their tricks."

"Great," Isaac said. "I'll carry you in a papoose."

He bolted from the room, but he was like a prisoner

in his glass house. Isaac's deputies began to arrive, one by one. J. Michael was flying in from Frisco, they said. Billy the Kid had called a press conference at Yankee Stadium in the afternoon.

"I can still shoot up to the Bronx, search for my son-in-law."

"Your Honor," said Nicholas Bright. "We have to strategize, or the Gov will get all the glory, and knock you out of the box in your own town."

They pawed at him, screamed, and Nicholas threatened to take his chopper away.

"I can do it, Isaac. Just zero your gas and oil allowance, put all your pilots on permanent sick leave."

"And I can fire you."

"But my instructions will still go into effect. That's the privilege of a first deputy mayor . . . you'll strategize with us until the conference, or we'll resign, and Billy the Kid can add City Hall to his other addresses."

He didn't want to go to the conference. He wasn't afraid of Billy. It was that chorus of Democrats—Seligman and Wooster and Porter Endicott. They had their own little war games.

His deputies sniffed at him. He'd been groping around for three days, living in his chopper with containers of Singapore noodles and vegetable dumplings, and he'd begun to stink. Martha Dime and Candy Cortez peeled off his clothes, sat him down in his tub, while Harvey selected his wardrobe with Nicholas Bright. He had to look like somebody who could pilot New York's bumpy ship of state. But Harve began to panic. The Big Guy had clinkers in his closet, rags that couldn't stand up to Billy the Kid's Armani suits. One of Harvey's pals appeared, a drunken tailor who'd dressed the Rockefellers forty years ago. He built a suit right on Isaac's back, banker's gray, with long pleats that made the Big Guy feel that he was trapped inside a kilt.

"Jesus," Isaac said, "everybody will laugh at me."

"Your Honor, it's beautiful," said Martha Dime. "It matches the color of your sideburns."

They read position papers to him. Isaac had a light lunch. "You can't let the Gov co-opt you," said Nicholas, who had a spy in Billy the Kid's camp. "He'll offer himself to the people once he declares how he helped settle the strike. He'll pose as the savior of the Bronx."

"That's ridiculous," Isaac said. "Billy wouldn't even lend us a nickel."

"It doesn't matter. He'll be at Yankee Stadium, in front of TV cameras, with half the planet watching him."

"He'll talk Bronx," said Martha Dime, "and he'll ass you right out of the picture."

"Then what can we do?"

"Give our support to the Bronx's internal programs."

"Like Sidereal," Isaac said, staring at Candida Cortez. "Fuck Billy the Kid."

They rode up to Yankee Stadium in the mayor's black sedan. Isaac sat between Candida and Dottie Dreamer, a political columnist for *Newsday*.

"Mr. Mayor," Dottie said, "there's been talk that you might move out of your mansion and into D.C."

"Not a chance," Isaac said. "There are too many mosquitoes in the Capital."

"But you're already a marked man," Dottie said, "the biggest vote getter in the Democratic arsenal."

"Come on, Dot. You can't have a president and vice-president from the same fucking state."

"Who knows? The Gov might not go down so well with the Party or the people."

Isaac had an anxiety attack. He should have stayed in the Bronx. Candida clutched his hand, whispered in his ear. "Brock has Barbarossa, but he's promised to give him back."

"Brock can't promise anything without consulting Billy the Kid."

They arrived at Yankee Stadium, climbed upstairs to the owners' box, which was cluttered with reporters and TV cameras and pols who stared at Isaac, admired his banker's gray. He shook hands with Billy the Kid and Michael Storm, who still had stubble on his face. Clarice was with him. The Yankees began to distribute champagne. The Bronx historian, Abner Gumm, moved about with his box camera. Isaac had to fight his own inclination to hurl Ab through the window. But the blue vein in his forehead began to pulse when he saw Brock Richardson. He sailed across the room to Brock.

"Where's Barbarossa?"

"Safe," Richardson said.

"I'll glock you the minute this conference is over."

"Glock Billy the Kid's personal guest? You can't touch me, Isaac. Stay out of my yard and you'll get Joey . . . in one piece."

"I'm closing Sidereal."

"Then you might as well close the Bronx... hey, I don't have time for this shit."

And Richardson pulled away from Isaac.

Billy the Kid held out his arms in front of the cameras, embraced Richardson and J. Michael Storm. "My two champions," he said, "my two courageous boys... ladies and gentlemen, what an afternoon for New York. J. Michael has given Yankee Stadium and every other ballpark in the land back to the people."

"What about us?" said Marvin Hatter, the Yankee president. "We deserve a little credit too."

"Shhh, Marvin. It's the people's day... the owners can start collecting tickets."

The pols clapped, and Billy gripped the microphone like some sexy crooner. "What about Richardson? He hasn't been locked up in any hotel room. He's made war on the worst gangs the City has ever seen, a prosecutor who doesn't sit on his fanny in some dark office, shining his shoes while the cases begin to pile up on his desk. Brock Richardson doesn't have a desk. His office is in the streets of the Bronx. He was appointed by our former police commissioner, Isaac Sidel, to win the Bronx back from those gangs, and win he did. But we're no primitive ward, ladies and gentlemen. Vengeance isn't our thing. I pledge myself to work with your mayor and Mr. Richardson to rebuild the Bronx..."

Isaac grew more and more morose. He walked out of Yankee Stadium in the middle of Billy's presidential speech.

23

It wasn't much fun to starve, particularly when Marianna could have ordered a whole duck with American Express. But she had to be loyal to Alyosha. And she had to endure all kinds of hissing.

—*Hey, homey, how's the puta, huh? You like her fruta bomba?*

He led her across the hills of a mangy park, where she almost slipped on a mama rat nursing her brood.

"Alyosha, take me out of here."

But he had nowhere to take her, just other streets, other parks, and when some lunatic leapt out of the dusk, Marianna had to whack him with her sword. The hissing multiplied.

—*Hey, maricón, you need downtown protection, huh? Can't even fight fair.*

Why couldn't they hail a cab with her American Express card and get out of this inferno of hills and rat babies? But Alyosha had his pride. He wouldn't abandon his native ground. *Homey* they called him. Marianna had lived in Houston and Dallas, but no one had ever said *homey* to her. She didn't have a native ground, wouldn't have known what it was. She had a lot of recipes, her aikido classes, and her pony, Lord Charles, who was on a ranch near Fort Worth, getting ancient without her. Lord Charles would probably grow a beard. She'd cried and cried, but Clarice said Manhattan wasn't a proper place for a horse. Marianna would need a bodyguard every time she rode Charles in Central Park. Charles was a sensitive beast. He might get stung by a wasp or develop asthma or get stolen by one of the Fantômases who lived in the park. But that wasn't the real reason. Clarice was selfish. She wouldn't pay to keep a horse in Manhattan.

—*Homey, when you gettin' married, huh?*

Marianna's arms grew weary of whacking so many lunatics.

"Couldn't we have a little vacation, homey?" she said to Alyosha.

"Vacation where?"

"You're the expert. We could picnic in the zoo, talk to the tigers."

"The Jokers would capture us and collect the reward money . . . I'll find you a gypsy cab."

"And leave you here in the woods?"

"Woods?" Alyosha said. "There aint no woods. We got the wilds, but that's different. The wilds is where tin cans and weeds can grow."

"Then I'll enjoy the wilds with you."

"We gotta run. The Dixie Cups are coming."

She carried the wooden sword in a sling around her shoulder and she couldn't run very far or very fast. Alyosha started to grab her hand when he saw Mouse's cousin, Felipe. And all of a sudden Alyosha didn't want to run. Felipe had surrounded himself with Dixie Cups, dreaming of rewards.

Alyosha twisted on his heels, pulled the sword out of Marianna's scabbard, and charged the Dixie Cups, who were terrified. They bit into their blackened pipes and disappeared, leaving Mouse's cousin all alone.

"I aint scared of you, bitch," Felipe shouted, but his eyes were wandering around in his head. Alyosha struck him across the chest, and Felipe collapsed, crumpled onto the ground.

"Don't kill, don't kill . . . I'm your homey."

Alyosha struck him again. Marianna didn't interfere. He wasn't robbing a five-year-old kid. He was attacking his own attackers.

"You aint my homey, and you never was."

Alyosha wanted to be a crusader and chop Felipe's head off, dismember him, fingers and all, but he could only smack with Marianna's wood, make Felipe black and blue. And after the third or fourth blow, he didn't have the same desire to punish. He wasn't a warrior. He was a runt who sprayed with cans and scratched with soft sticks.

"Felipe, if you'd treated me better at Spofford, the Mouse and my brother would still be alive. I gave your cousin to the Apaches, hear? . . . who am I, huh?"

"The mightiest little man in the Bronx."

All the vengeance had gone out of Alyosha. He

wanted his brother back, he wanted Paul. He dropped the sword and Felipe ran away, returned to whatever wildland he'd come out of, a wildland that was and wasn't the Bronx, because a wind blew inside Alyosha's head that was much more savage than any borough. He was sick to death of Dixie Cups and blackened pipes and the little torches that warmed up white coal. He'd never be another Rembrandt. He could only draw dunes.

Marianna picked up the sword and thrust it into her scabbard, while Alyosha wandered into the middle of the street. He was like a sleepwalker who couldn't find his way home. He didn't have a home without Paulito. Marianna had to bump him out of the path of ambulances and a bus that had no passengers. A gypsy cab stopped for them. Marianna got into the cab with her artist. "Sutton Place South," she said.

The driver wore dark glasses and carried a Glock inside his waistband. "Where's that, little mama?"

"Over the bridge." That's the only knowledge she had about the line between Manhattan and the Bronx. The driver knew that gypsies weren't welcome in Manhattan, that the other hacks would scream at him and smash his windows if he didn't get in and out. But he liked the little mama and her sword and the catatonic boy she was with. He delivered them to Sutton Place South.

"Do you take American Express?" Marianna asked the driver.

"Not lately," he said. "But I'll tell you what . . . lend

me your sword. I'll give it back in a month. What's
your name?"

"Marianna."

"Good. I'll leave it with the doorman."

She gave up her sword and hustled Alyosha out of
the cab, brought him upstairs. Clarice was having dinner on the terrace. Vodka and cold potato pie.
"Lovely," she said. "My two favorite Merlins . . . what's
wrong with him? He looks like he fell off a ship."

"Mother, haven't you noticed? I've been gone for
three days."

"Impossible," Clarice said. "Didn't I see you brushing
your teeth last night?"

"No," Marianna said. "It must have been Fantômas."

"How dare you run away and not even tell your
mother."

"I didn't run away. I collected Alyosha."

"He isn't collectable. Does he look like a toy?"

A tear settled under Marianna's eye. She grabbed the
vodka bottle away from Clarice, ordered her out of the
terrace, and put her to bed. It wasn't even six P.M., but
Clarice curled up and started to snore. And then Marianna thought of a treat for Alyosha and herself. She
whipped up some batter in an enormous bowl, prepared her old standard, mocha chip. And while the
cookies ripened in the oven, she climbed into the
shower with Alyosha, and she wasn't ashamed of re-
vealing herself. She kissed him under that storm of
water, and his dark blue eyes seemed to notice her
nakedness.

"Alyosha, don't be afraid."

"Merlin," he said. That was the only sound he made, and Marianna would have kissed him for hours if she hadn't smelled the burning batter. She abandoned Alyosha for a minute and ran in to save her cookies.

24

Mimi Brothers was outside the Castle Motel, chatting with Abner Gumm on her radio. "Shooter, it's a dead night . . . I can't even feed any of the girls. Wait a second. I think I found a john. He looks kind of funny, like a chicken that floated in from Wall Street."

She'd sucked on too many pipes with the other girls. Her eyes had gotten bleary. She didn't recognize the john in the banker's suit until he was close enough to cover the mouth of her radio. It was Sidel, wearing the only disguise that could have fooled Nurse Mimi Brothers. Without his baggy pants, he looked like any other mayor.

"Mimi, tell Ab to come on out."

"And what if I won't?" she said.

"Then I'll lock you in your nurse's van for the rest of your fucking life."

"You wouldn't dare," Mimi said. "You don't have the balls . . . I could knock you flat on your ass."

He might have had pity for the godmother at a whore's motel, but this godmother was Abner's spy. She flexed her muscles, revealed the tattoo on her left bicep. *Heart of Gold.* The three words began to wiggle. She was hoping to crack the Big Guy in the head while he watched the tattoo, drag him into the van, and deal with him any way the Shooter wanted. But the Big Guy grabbed her fist and squeezed with both hands. The nurse howled. She was still clutching the radio.

"Call him," Isaac whispered.

"Shooter," she rasped into the radio. "I have a cash problem. Will ya meet me at the van?"

Isaac heard the Shooter growl, "I'm busy, babe . . . right in the middle of my nap."

"It will only take a sec."

The Shooter marched out of the motel in his bathrobe and slippers. Isaac stood behind the nurse, obscured by her bulk. The blood rushed into his temples. His blue vein was pulsing like mad. He didn't have to play Fantômas. He *was* the king of crime. He took the Shooter and tossed him into the van with Mimi Brothers. The stink sickened him. The van smelled of rotting chocolate and rat turds. That was Mimi's atmosphere.

She reached for one of her baseball bats. Isaac had to clip her on the forehead, and she fell into the Shooter's arms. "Mr. Mayor, have you gone out of your mind?"

"Shut up. Ab, you've been milking the Bronx for fifty years, ever since you inherited that box camera. It was never a hobby. It was a fucking poisonous vocation. Who was your first subject, Ab? Tell the truth?"

"Naked girls," the Shooter said. "I stood outside their bathroom window, on the fire escape, photographed them before they got into the tub. It was grand. Isaac, isn't that what you'd say?"

"Never mind what I'd say. You sold the pictures, huh?"

"To every man and boy in the neighborhood."

"You were the Bronx Audubon, a bird watcher . . . but you graduated from bathroom windows, didn't you, Ab? You ranged the Bronx with your camera, walked everywhere, old, reliable Ab, the infant prodigy. You hooked up with the gangs, became their watchman."

"It was my own idea," the Shooter said. "Who would ever suspect me? An innocent with a child's camera. I could climb under any police cordon, warn a gang when the bulls were coming."

"Ah, but it was only pennies . . . until crack came along."

"Isaac, I didn't invent drugs."

"But you did work for the Bronx brigade."

"Of course. You couldn't last one day in the Bronx without Brock Richardson. I had to climb aboard."

"And you danced between him and the Dominicans."

"Brock had already massacred the local gangs. He needed the Dominoes. Martin Lima was the only one who had any cash."

"And you, Ab?"

"I'm struggling," the Shooter said. "I have holes in my pants, like the mayor of New York."

"Then you must be blind, even with your camera. I'm wearing a million-dollar suit, Persian wool."

"It's the clothes of a candidate."

"Shut up," Isaac said. "Where's Barbarossa?"

"You think I have him inside the motel? Take a look. I'll even lend you a piece of ass."

Isaac tapped him once on the skull. "Where's Barbarossa?"

"Richardson has him. I'm not privy to his secrets. I do portraits for him. I'm the house photographer."

Isaac tapped him again. "We can do this all day. Ab, where's Barbarossa?"

"At Claremont Village," the Shooter said.

"I'm a baby," Isaac muttered, giving himself a wicked slap on the head. "Claremont Village . . . Richardson doesn't need any other roost. It's the one place I would never have bothered to search. That fucker is in league with African Dave."

"It's not Dave's fault. The other warlords on the roof were ganging up against him. He had to go to Richardson. The Apaches threatened to burn down Claremont Village and start smoking warlords off the roof. They have no scruples. Dave's own children would have died."

"Dave's a bachelor," Isaac said. "All the warlords are. They're like a bunch of nomads on that roof."

"They're still family men," the Shooter insisted. "Dave himself has six wives. I had a session with the entire brood. Should I show you?"

"Shut up. You're taking me to Barbarossa. You're gonna walk me right up to the roof."

"In my bathrobe? It's almost winter."

"I'll hug you, Ab. I'll keep you warm."

"But lemme get my camera. I can't travel without that box. I get the shakes. I'll tell Dave that I'm coming to photograph Barbarossa."

"Good," Isaac said. "You'll photograph him without your camera."

He tied up the nurse with a ratty piece of rope, stuffed two stockings into her mouth, kicked Abner Gumm out of the van, marched him across the Grand Concourse and down the hill to Claremont Village and its merciless regimen of lights, like half-dead eyes in an endless world.

The Shooter had never been this long without his box camera. He lost all sense of harmony, the musical call that kept him alive, his own special rapture when he clicked and clicked. He had to frame things, catch the world through the eye of his camera or else he wasn't happy.

"Isaac, I'm sinking," he said. "I won't be coherent enough to help."

"Not to worry. I'll build a fire in your ass. The words will come."

They stood in the central garden, among the demolished playpens; not even the huge concrete turtles that had been built into the ground like reptilian gods could withstand the ravages of Claremont Village; their noses and eyes and legs had been chopped off; their shells had become a porous powder: these turtles were bald. Isaac wondered how many children had climbed onto the turtles' backs. They were the most dependable creatures in the project.

He nudged the Shooter. "Wave," he said. "This is your country, not mine. I'm an uninvited guest."

The Shooter managed to smile. "I'm shocked. This is City housing. Claremont is your country."

"Wave, Shooter, or I'll let you sleep with the turtles."

The Shooter waved. Suddenly he and Isaac were drowned in searchlights, like two men caught in a colorless rainbow. "It's all right," the Shooter said. "They recognize us." He darted out of the rainbow with Isaac, but the elevators were broken, and they had to climb nineteen flights; both of them were dizzy when they landed on the roof.

Barbarossa was handcuffed to a lead chair, the kind that was used at precincts to prevent prisoners from running off like wild turkeys with whatever furniture they were chained to. Richardson must have supplied African Dave with the chair. Two teen-aged girls were sitting in his lap, fondling Barbarossa while they smoked their little pipes. They both had Glocks inside their garters. Isaac recognized Martin Lima's crack babies who tore up the Bronx from inside a white Cadillac. The prince himself was a pockmarked boy worth millions of dollars. He wore an Italian suit, like Billy the Kid. Isaac had never talked to the wizard. Martin Lima was smoking crack with African Dave, who clutched his portable searchlight with one hand, wheeled it here and there, as if he could read the sky.

"Dave," Isaac said, "will you ask the girls to stop

kissing Barbarossa. He's a married man. His wife wouldn't like it."

"El Caballo," Martin Lima said, almost shy. "You'll have to ask me . . . the girls are mine."

Isaac bowed to the prince. "Please . . ."

"Miranda, Dolores, get away. You're bothering the son-in-law of El Caballo."

"We like him, papito," Miranda said. "We love him. We want to be his esposa."

"Are you deaf? Don't insult him. He's a married man."

"Papito," Dolores said, "buy him for me."

"Niñas, this is El Caballo. He will grow angry at me."

"But we are the ones who sleep in your bed, papito, not him."

Martin Lima struck the girls, drove them from Barbarossa's lap.

"I spoil them, El Caballo. Forgive me."

Now Isaac could see the welts and marks on Barbarossa's face. He wanted to glock everybody, including the crack babies and Abner Gumm. But he had to be as cold as the king of crime.

"Uncuff him, will ya?"

"It's tragic, El Caballo, but I don't have the key. It belongs to the Apaches . . . hey, Shooter, why are you here?"

"To take Barbarossa's picture."

"That's nice," Martin Lima said, and never even noticed the Shooter's missing camera. The Big Guy had been right: Ab's camera had become something you imagined when you imagined Ab.

"Joey," Isaac said, "you okay?"

"Yeah, Dad," Barbarossa said. "My tongue was bleeding, but it stopped. It tastes like salt."

"Príncipe, will you reach into your pocket and find your portable phone . . . ask Brock to bring the key."

"Brock doesn't have it. I do."

Isaac peeked behind him. Birdy Towne dragged himself along in his boots and mustard-colored pants, like a damaged cowboy with a crutch under one arm. He'd arrived with Richardson, who was wearing a long coat.

"What happened, Birdy? Did you step on a live alligator?"

"Naw. It's much more bitter than that. Your little cookie baker slapped me while I wasn't looking. With a goddamn wooden sword. She was protecting that mural boy."

"Shit," Isaac said. He'd forgotten all about Alyosha. His mind was a swamp. He couldn't even save one of his own Merliners. All he could do was invent mustard-colored cowboys who were eating up the Bronx. "Where are they, Birdy?"

"Romeo and Juliet? Picking their belly buttons. We'll find them . . . like we found you. The Shooter's part of our radar. We tracked him the minute he left the motel."

"Yeah," Isaac said, "he's my very own Virgil."

"Isaac, you have a problem. You read too many books . . . this man taught me everything I know. He's the greatest teacher in New York. But he thinks the world is filled with men in masks who are always running around on roofs, huh Joey?"

"We're on a roof right now," Barbarossa said.

"That's because the Big Guy's whole life leads up to a roof. But we aint wearing masks."

"Shove it, Birdy," Richardson said. "Shut your mouth."

"Ah," Isaac said, "he was my slowest pupil, and look how far he's gotten . . . Príncipe, have you said your prayers?"

"Prayers? What for?"

"Birdy can't whack me and Barbarossa without whacking you."

"Hey," Birdy said, "who says . . ."

Martin Lima glared at him. "Let El Caballo finish his speech."

"I'm too dangerous to be alive. I'll haunt Richardson into the ground. I'll bust his whole brigade. And he has ambitions. He'd like to go into politics, but he can't until he murders me."

Martin Lima started to laugh while he picked his teeth. "Birdy's right. You are a storyteller, and I'm the Bronx's only banker. Richardson works for me. He couldn't survive without my gelt. I'm the one who can afford to kill people, and why should I kill El Caballo?"

"Príncipe, you should have gone to my classes at the Academy. Brock will have a bigger banker. Uncle Sam. He'll borrow from Uncle once Billy the Kid is in the White House. Meanwhile I get caught in the crossfire. The mayor and his son-in-law are bopped in the thick of battle, while Brock Richardson shuts down the biggest drug depot in the Bronx. Claremont Village. It will sell a lot of newspapers, Príncipe. I'm the former PC. It's logical that I'd show up on a roof with Brock."

"And what about Dave and the warlords? They're gonna be idle in this bump?"

"They're already idle. They lost their independence once they agreed to become your depot. The warlords are holding for you and Brock. What are they? Clowns with searchlights."

"Who's a clown?" asked African Dave, his mouth already blackened from the pipe. He followed the beam of his searchlight, a strange, liquid arc that could fold into the sky, and he plucked a machine pistol from behind the casing of the light and pointed it at Isaac. But the prince floated across the roof with his portly frame and kicked the gun out of Dave's hands. "No cannons, Dave. We could have an unlucky accident . . . go back to your light." And the prince returned to Sidel. "I'm in command. Ask Brock."

Brock was busy with the roach in his mouth; bits of grass dropped into his fingers. Isaac was curious about Richardson's long mustard-colored coat: it was like the coat a cowboy would wear to protect him from wind and dust. "He's the prince," Brock said. "I'm just an employee."

"Don't you get it?" Martin Lima implored the Big Guy. "We had to grab your son-in-law."

"Why?"

"To bring you to the bargaining table. Live and let live, that's my motto. You want culture? I'll contribute. Two hundred thousand marbles to the Merliners, whoever they are. I'm not selfish. The Bronx is big enough for you and me and Brock."

"Uncuff Barbarossa."

"But will you sign with us, El Caballo?"

"Uncuff him first."

The prince whispered to one of his crack babies, who approached Birdy Towne, swiped a little key from his pocket, stood behind the prisoner's chair, and freed Barbarossa.

Birdy pulled out his Glock. "He has to sit there. He can't move."

"Brock," the prince shouted, "tell Birdy to holster up."

"Boss," Birdy said, "you can't trust the Big Guy. He's unreliable. He'll take Barbarossa and he'll never stop hounding us . . . let's sock both of them, like you said."

"Shut your mouth," Richardson told him.

"Brock," the prince said, "who's the planner? Me or you?"

"I'm the planner," Isaac said.

The prince started to bark. "Stay out of this. You sleep in Manhattan. This is our show."

"Wrong," Isaac said. "The Apaches are mine. Brock is mine. And so are you. I'm the landlord. I own everything. Claremont Village. Yankee Stadium. Everything."

"Mister," the prince said, "I checked out your finances. You're two minutes from the poorhouse."

"I'm still the landlord."

"Prince," Brock said, while the roach started to unravel. "He's the man. He's our landlord."

"I'm killing Barbarossa," Birdy said. "I don't care."

The prince signaled to his crack babies, who reached for the Glocks in their garters. But Richardson pulled a Nighthawk out of his long coat and shot Miranda and Dolores. The prince was mortified. "Dave," he said, "do something."

Isaac jumped on Barbarossa, toppled him in that lead chair, pulled him out of the line of fire . . . as tracer bullets arrived from across the roof, like miraculous glowworms with a busy sting. The other warlords must have decided to attack. It was Claremont Village, which had its own rules.

Birdy kept aiming at the hump of Isaac's back while the tracers flew around him. Richardson shot Birdy and Prince Martin Lima. Isaac couldn't stop looking. He'd never encountered such a lethal glass gun.

Dave fired back at the warlords. "Son of a bitch."

"Boss," Richardson said, "we'd better blow."

Isaac should have glocked him. It would have been a slightly extra load to all the carnage. But he kept thinking of Candida Cortez and the baby she was carrying. Brock was a bigger delinquent than the Latin Jokers or the San Juan Freaks, but he was *Isaac's* delinquent.

"Dad, should I strangle him?" Barbarossa whispered in Isaac's ear.

"No. We'll find a way to ruin the fuck."

They crawled among the dead bodies and Dave's shattered rooftop furniture when they noticed Abner Gumm. The Shooter sat close to Dave and Dave's light, with his fingers curled, forming the eye of a camera. "Mama," he said, "it's like Vietnam."

Barbarossa dragged him away from the searchlight. "What do you know about Nam? You scumbag, you've never been north of the Bronx."

"Joey," the Shooter kept saying, "the light, the light . . . those bullets were scratching my eyeballs. I felt it, man."

Barbarossa hit him in the mouth and carried him off the roof behind Sidel and Brock Richardson, who'd already buttoned up his mustard-colored coat.

25

Cameramen appeared from all over the planet. Isaac couldn't destroy the myth that had surrounded him: the mayor of New York had rescued his son-in-law from Claremont Village, the worst badland in the Bronx. The Big Guy would walk into a gangster's den and come out alive, sneeze in the middle of a firestorm, survive tapeworms and knocks on the head. He was only scared of one man: Sweets. The PC wouldn't tap-dance with politicians, wouldn't take Isaac's shit.

The Big Guy had to run down to Police Plaza. He knew that Sweets was going to raid Claremont Village, "neutralize" the warlords with his sharpshooters from Emergency Services. They had elephant guns and armored trucks and impenetrable shields. Isaac rode up to the fourteenth floor and waited in Sweets' vestibule for half an hour. Finally Sweets ducked out of his office. He was six feet four, and could make Isaac feel like a fucking dwarf in his presence. "You're not going to Claremont Village with ESU."

"Sweets, can't we argue in your office?"

Isaac entered the office where he'd lived for five years and which Sweets had inherited from him, with Teddy Roosevelt's desk and the same jungle plants.

"I'll arrest you if you go near my tactical team. Claremont is off-limits."

"But couldn't I watch the action from my chopper?"

"No choppers," Sweets said. "Those mothers have all kinds of military hardware. They'll shoot you right out of the sky."

"Who's leading the assault?"

"I am. With Brock Richardson and ESU."

"Brock?" Isaac said.

"The Bronx is his domain. I can't leave him out of the picture."

"He was working with the warlords. He slept on that roof."

"He's your baby," Sweets said. "I'll throw him to Internal, but not until I take Claremont Village."

"Sweets, let me come with you as an observer. I won't draw. You can have my Glock."

Sweets gazed into Isaac's miserable eyes. "You'll stick behind the shields?"

"I promise."

"And you'll wear a vest?"

"I'm the mayor. I'll look ridiculous with fiberglass under my coat . . . I'll wear the vest."

He rode into the Bronx with Sweets. ESU had already assembled in Claremont's common garden, near the wounded turtles. They were all carrying elephant guns. They looked like gladiators under their helmets and shields. Richardson wore a bulletproof vest. He held Sweets' horn to his lips and shouted at the roof. "African Dave, this is your last chance to surrender. Give up your weapons and come downstairs. I repeat. Give up your weapons and—"

Tracers struck the turtles and the shields; the warlords shone their lights in the gladiators' eyes, blinded the whole tactical team. Isaac was stranded in a red wall of light. But the gladiators raised their shields into the glare and rushed the main building. Isaac followed them up the stairs, galloping like they did, a couple of steps at a time. The warlords had barricaded the door to the roof, but ESU broke it down with sledgehammers and stepped onto the roof. African Dave stood on the far side of his own little Copacabana with several warlords, their wives and children in front of them.

"Sweets," Richardson said, "it's pathetic. Exploiting women and children, using them as shields. Should I parley with the fuckers?"

But a chopper appeared above Copacabana. It didn't belong to ESU. Isaac laughed into his own fist. Richardson must have told Billy the Kid about the raid, and Billy had to ride over the battlefield like some deus ex machina, the man who would be president. "This is the governor," he screamed into his microphone. "Clear the area immediately . . . lay down your arms."

Sweets put his hands over his eyes and rocked his head . . . as the warlords concentrated all their firepower on Billy the Kid. The chopper's tail fell off; the machine shivered in the wind, and plunged into the garden between two turtles. Sweets' backup team had to rescue Billy, pull him out of the burning machine.

"Hey, boys, how you like that?" African Dave shouted from behind his wall of women. "Who's next?"

Isaac crept between two of the shields and started to cross Copacabana. "Isaac," Sweets said, "you broke your promise. Will you get back?"

"I promised to stand and watch a fight, not a slaughter, Sweets."

The warlords didn't fire at El Caballo. The children hadn't washed their faces. Isaac looked into their eyes, touched their foreheads, and walked up to Dave. "You're no warrior. You're not even a nihilist. You're outside my fucking respect." He slapped Dave in front of women, children, and warlords. "Come on. Pulverize me, Dave. Prove what a hero you are."

"We had to mobilize all the bitches," Dave said. "Richardson was coming with his death squad."

"This aint Richardson's show," Isaac said. "Dave, come with me."

The warlords dropped their weapons and crossed Copacabana with Isaac the Brave.

Sweets' men discovered a mountain of crack and sixteen million dollars in small bills, strewn among diapers and baby shit. Reporters marched through Claremont Village, interviewed twelve-year-old children who'd never gone to school. "David Copperfield," they scribbled. "Oliver Twist." Democratic hopefuls visited "this sewer and sink of the Western World," but Sidel had already been there, Sidel had captured the warlords without wearing a gun. Dottie Dreamer of *Newsday* kept talking about the *late* Billy the Kid. "There'll be a new political marriage. That's my guess." And then a photo appeared in *Newsday* of the Gov in a sordid position. Billy was being whipped by a woman who wasn't his wife. The photo had a familiar sting; Isaac could almost tell whose eye had observed Billy the Kid. Abner Gumm had climbed the fire escape of some hotel to catch Billy the Kid with a call girl.

The Big Guy began to worry. His name was tied to Michael Storm. "A dream ticket," Dottie said. "The experienced son backed by his spiritual dad. Michael Storm, who ended an ugly baseball war, and Isaac Sidel, the passionate policeman (and mayor) who risked his own life to spare the abused children of Claremont Village. The Republican Party will have to ride on some camel and run to the ends of the earth."

Isaac wouldn't take Dottie Dreamer's calls. He removed himself from reporters and Party hacks. He didn't even have Bernardo Dublin to bark at. Bernardo moved out of the back bedroom while Isaac had gone to the Bronx with Sweets. Isaac couldn't console himself with Marianna's cookies. She was baking for her house guest, Alyosha. But neither of them had invited him downtown for potato chips on the terrace.

"They've forgotten me," he said. "They're kids . . . they have their own lives. What did Birdy say? Romeo and Juliet."

And then the baseball czar called. "Isaac, we have to chat."

"I don't think so, J."

"I'll expect you at six."

He didn't have the heart to visit J. alone. He brought Barbarossa, whose face was still black-and-blue (no one could recover very fast from one of Birdy's beatings). Clarice met them at the door.

"Where's Alyosha?" he asked.

"I'm not sure. He mopes a lot. He's hardly a communicative boy."

"He's mourning his brother. And he hasn't been able to do a mural."

"He could decorate the whole apartment. I wouldn't care."

Bernardo was in the living room with J. and Tim Seligman. Bernardo could have been Barbarossa's twin brother. They were both black and blue.

"Where's Alyosha."

"Don't dodge the issue," Seligman said. "That's not why you're here. We can't run you for President. There's the Jewish problem. But if we turn the order around? With an Episcopalian on top, and you right behind, we can't miss. The adventurous son and the law and order dad to quiet him."

"J. isn't my son."

"Isaac, we're talking metaphors. You molded J."

"And what if I decide not to run?"

"J. wouldn't work without you. But did I forget to mention that Margaret Tolstoy is in D.C.?"

"I thought she was in Prague, living with some cultural attaché?"

"We had to move her, Isaac. She was getting too popular . . . she's involved with a Romanian general."

"And you'll let me see her if I'm a good boy."

"We'll withdraw the general, send him to Bucharest."

"So I can have my dangerous liaison."

"There's no danger," Seligman said.

"Then why can't I see Margaret while I'm mayor?"

"We already talked about it," Seligman said, rolling his eyes. "You live in a glass house. But as vice-president, you'll be on the back burner . . . Isaac, the Party needs you. You can't pedal backwards once you enter politics."

"All right. Then assassinate Brock Richardson for me. I mean it. If your friends won't do it, Joey will cancel him for me."

"Your Honor," J. said, "will you be a little more discreet? If we're bugging the Republicans, they could be bugging us."

"And what does the Grand Old Party say about Sidel?"

"Dynamite. They're frightened to death."

"J., how did you end the strike? What did you promise the owners that got them to cave in?"

"Nothing. I said that when I was done with politics I'd consider becoming the commissioner of baseball."

"That's brilliant. You fuck both sides without fucking yourself. And what happens to Sidereal when Tim Seligman puts you in the White House?"

"There won't be any complications. Porter's bank

will buy up all our family shares, and the money will go into a blind trust."

"Perfect," Isaac said. "A blind trust. And how much money will mama, papa, and Marianna have made off Sidereal?"

"Peanuts," J. said. "Presidents don't need pocket money."

"Grand."

"You can't kill Brock. He's one of your children. We all came out from under your overcoat. Isn't that what Tolstoy said about Pushkin? Remind me, Isaac. You were our teacher."

"Your batteries are crossed, J. It was Dostoyevsky talking about Gogol and his genius for inventing ghosts. But I don't have the same overcoat."

"Yes you do. You put Richardson in place, him and those other bandits . . . we're gonna run him for congress in the South Bronx."

"And it doesn't matter, J., that he murdered children?"

"We're still running him. The case is closed."

"Boss, I came out from under the overcoat," Bernardo said, sitting near Clarice. "With Barbarossa."

"What's Bernardo doing here?"

"He's Clarice's new bodyguard," J. said. "I'm borrowing him from the Bronx brigade."

Bernardo must have been Clarice's consolation prize. She'd play the candidate's wife if Bernardo could come along. J. wouldn't have to spy on his wife. He'd know exactly which bed she was in.

Marianna came into the room looking glum. "Uncle

Isaac, mom and dad wouldn't let me come to the mansion. They said I had to leave you alone. You couldn't spend so much time with a little girl."

"Where's Alyosha?"

"He ran away. He loves me but he hates Manhattan."

"Don't talk foolish," Clarice said. "He couldn't stay here. He's a convict."

"You can't call a twelve-year-old kid a convict. He was in a juvenile facility. It's medieval. But it's not a jail. Now if you'll excuse me, I'd like to find Alyosha . . . can I borrow your daughter, J.?"

"Ask Clarice."

"She's silly. But take her if you want."

"What about our deal?" Seligman said.

"I'll think about it. I can't make snap decisions. I'm only a guy who lives in a glass house."

And Isaac left with Marianna and his son-in-law.

"Where's your sword?"

"A gypsy cabdriver borrowed it. He promised to bring it back."

They got into Isaac's limousine, and the Big Guy listened to the police radio, switched from band to band. There was a new vigilante in the Bronx, called himself the Good Knight. He appeared in different neighborhoods, attacked local stickup artists with some kind of sword. Isaac caught the story on his scanner.

. . . EMS transporting three young Hispanic males on land to Bronx Hospital. They all have multiple bruises and were carrying guns and knives. A witness who won't give her name says they tried to rob a bodega at one-three-five Grand Concourse, and a male Hispanic with a sword disarmed them and drove away . . . no make on the sword. Must be the Good Knight . . . what you got? . . . Yankee Stadium, large commotion . . . young Hispanic male is defacing a whole lot of wall . . . should I get it?

Barbarossa raced up to Yankee Stadium with his siren on. It was like the old days, when Isaac was PC and Joe had just started to court Marilyn the Wild. The Big Guy was born to make trouble, not to govern. He felt like dancing in the street. There was a crowd in front of the stadium. Isaac had to laugh. He was almost happy . . . without Margaret Tolstoy. He discovered an enormous image on the stadium's southern wall. Paulito Carpenteros wearing the blue handkerchief hat of the Latin Jokers. And Alyosha hadn't placed Paul inside any idyllic backdrop. He'd recreated the Bronx, *his* Bronx, from the Third Avenue Bridge, with blue sharks feeding in the water, to Yankee Stadium and the Castle Motel and a little hobby shop on Jerome Avenue with a demonic face in the window; from the Cross Bronx, which looked like a gigantic dead snake, to Claremont Village and Crotona Park; the rest of the borough was one long Sahara with a building here and there and endless dunes.

PAULITO CARPENTEROS, LORD OF THE SOUTH BRONX
REST IN PEACE, GENERAL
PAID FOR BY THE LATIN JOKERS WAR FUND

Isaac got out of the car with Joe and Marianna

Storm. He had to lunge into the crowd, and when people asked him for his autograph, he grunted, "Not now." Two patrolmen arrived. They stood with Marvin Hatter, the Yankee president, near Alyosha, who looked like a glass boy on his own little ladder.

"Thank God," said Marvin Hatter. "Isaac, I don't want to see that kid arrested, but we can't have graffiti on our walls."

"That's not graffiti, Marvin. It's a war memorial."

"We still can't have it here."

"I'm the landlord, Marvin. The memorial stays."

Marvin Hatter stared into the crowd, appraised all the interest in Alyosha's art, shook Isaac's hand, and disappeared with the patrolmen.

The Big Guy found himself on the wall. The kid had painted him with blue sideburns and a slight hump. The Bronx wasn't such a Sahara. There were other people hidden in the dunes, like a little family: Isaac recognized Richardson with a roach in his mouth, Marianna with her big medallion, Marilyn the Wild, Bernardo Dublin wearing a mask, Martin Lima and his crack babies, Miranda and Dolores . . . Isaac had never even mourned those two little girls. The Big Guy was ashamed of himself.

Alyosha came down off his ladder. He'd been working for eight hours and was hungry as hell. Marianna put her arms around him. "You shouldn't have run away . . . I was worried."

"I had to do Paulito," Alyosha said. "And this was the only wall that was big enough. Now every homey who comes to see a Yankee game will remember Paul."

Isaac didn't know what he'd do with Alyosha. Adopt

him, name him the new Bronx historian? "Joey," he said, "will you go to a deli and get us some sandwiches?"

"We don't need sandwiches," Marianna said, and took a batch of cookies out of her bag.

Alyosha bit into a cookie. It wasn't peanut brittle or mocha chip.

"Rum raisin," Marianna said. "A new recipe . . ."

And Alyosha mounted the ladder again. He still had to draw the model planes in David Six Fingers' shop. Rest in Peace, Homey. The Big Jew could put him in jail. Alyosha didn't care. But he just couldn't live without his ladder.

"Uncle Joe," he said to Barbarossa, "where's the Big Guy gonna take me?"

"Somewhere," Barbarossa said. "We'll see."

They watched Isaac for some signal.

"Alyosha." Isaac had nothing more to say. He couldn't hide a glass boy in a glass house. Both of them might break. And then he looked deeper into the design on the wall: Alyosha had included Gracie Mansion, sat it on a little dune between Claremont Village and Crotona Park; it had chimneys and porches, but this glass house didn't face the sea; it looked out upon all the other dunes, like some ghostly lighthouse. The Big Guy hopped around the ladder, with his own crazy joy. Alyosha was absorbing Manhattan bit by bit. Isaac didn't have to abandon his glass house. He could live in it with Alyosha, call it the Bronx.